THE
SILVER
HORSE

THE
SILVER
HORSE

Elizabeth A. Lynn

BLUEJAY BOOKS INC.

A Bluejay Book, published by arrangement with the Author.
Copyright © 1984 by Elizabeth A. Lynn
Jacket painting by Victoria Poyser
Author sketch and interior illustrations by Jeanne Gomoll
Book design by Terry McCabe

Manufactured in the United States of America
First Bluejay Printing: August 1984

Library of Congress Cataloging in Publication Data

Lynn, Elizabeth A.
    The silver horse.

Summary: Eleven-year old Susannah follows her brother and his
beautiful silver horse to the Land of Lost Toys, where she finds herself
in the middle of a fantastic adventure.
    1. Children's stories, American. [1. Fantasy. 2. Toys—Fiction.
3. Lost and found possessions—Fiction] I. Title.
PZ7.L992Si 1984   [Fic]   84-18609
ISBN 0-312-94404-7

The author appreciates the encouragement and assistance of David Primo D'Aluiso, Kevin Arjuna Knight, Misty Star Gottlieb, Debbie Notkin, Jim Frenkel, and Laurence Yep.

For the two Susans

Jeanne Gomoll

Chapter One

Susannah sat looking out her bedroom window at the park.

You're too old to play with toys, she told herself silently. *Much too old.*

Beyond the green square park she could just see the skyscrapers of San Francisco. They seemed shiny and clean against the sky of brilliant blue. Sometimes Susannah could look at them and pretend that they were not steel skyscrapers but silver and gold and crystal towers.

Not today, she thought. They look like fence posts today.

Her nose itched, the way it did when she wanted to cry and wouldn't. Rubbing it, she turned her back to the window and looked across the room. Her brother's purple toy chest sat beside his bed, lid down. The wooden silver horse—Niall was crazy about horses—stood on top.

The horse had been a birthday present. Susannah's best friend's mother, Celie, had found it in a thrift store, scraped it clean of its flaking black paint and repainted it with silver glitter. As its proud mane and arrogant pricked ears caught the light, they sparkled like sunshine on the sea. It had only been in the house three days, but it made Susannah's things—her checked bedspread, her pictures on the wall, even the bright fantastic jackets on her books—look shabby.

Niall was so pleased with it that he had stuffed all his other toys out of sight.

There was one thing in the room the horse couldn't make shabby. Crossing to her bed, Susannah reached beneath it and pulled out her new paint box. She had saved her allowance money all year and had bought it for herself. Her parents had bought her a real sable brush to go with it. It had forty colors in it. There had only been twelve colors in her old paint box.

Hugging the paint box, Susannah walked to the horse. I bet I could draw you, she told it. Horses were hard to draw. The difficult part would be the head, with all the delicate detail of lips and eyes and ears. It would be hard, too, to show the way the muscles ran on the graceful arching neck. The musculature, Susannah repeated to herself. She had just learned the word. The horse had very clear musculature.

Niall wandered into the room. "What are you doing?" he

whined. Without waiting for her answer, he shouted, "Ma, Susannah's bothering my horse!"

"I'm not bothering your old horse," Susannah said. "How could I bother him, he's just wood!" Shoving the new paint box under the bed, she jammed her fists into her pockets and went into the hallway. She had made a secret vow that she wouldn't fight with Niall, no matter how snotty he was, for a week after his birthday, and she knew if she stayed in the bedroom she would break her promise.

Had she been that snotty when she was six years old?

She doubted it. But when she was six, Niall was one year old. He was kind of cute then. And they hadn't had to share a room; he had slept in her parents' room, in a crib. One thing you could say about school; in school they didn't have to be together the whole day as they were now. Almost Susannah regretted that there was no school.

But she didn't want to be in school. She just wanted *Niall* to be in school.

The door at the end of the hallway was open a little. "Mother?" she said.

"I'm here," said her mother's voice from the other side of the door. Susannah pulled the door further open and stuck her head around it. Her mother turned around. "Hey," she said. "Come outside."

Susannah slid through the opening. Her mother was sitting on the top landing with her feet on the steps. Carefully, because the steps were splintery and because she was barefoot, Susannah climbed down two steps, sat, and leaned against her mother's legs.

Her mother's name was Bonnie. She was tall, with golden hair that she wore in braids or piled on top of her head. She liked to cook and she liked to dance. But she hadn't gone out dancing in a long time, because she was going to have a baby. She had been going to have a baby since Christmas. Susannah had heard her say once to Celie that she liked having babies, she liked the feel of being pregnant. Celie, who had been pregnant at the time, said, "I don't!" Susannah didn't think she would like it much, walking around all puffed out in front and not wearing blue jeans.

But she wondered what it felt like, being pregnant.

Her mother skipped her fingers over the top of Susannah's head. "Hey, Susie-pooh. How you doing?"

"Okay," Susannah said. She rested her chin on her arms. "Mother?"

"Hmm?"

"When will the baby come out?" She had been told. But it was hard for her sometimes to keep track of months.

"In September. This is June. June to July, July to August, August to September." She walked her fingers over the top of Susannah's head again. "A Virgo kid."

Susannah knew what that meant, sort of. It meant that the planets and stars that were in the sky the day you were born made you act in certain ways as you got older. Mother read about it in the paper every morning.

Susannah had asked Mr. Gonzalez, her teacher, about astrology. He had said that the stars and planets were so far away that they couldn't make anyone do anything.

Susannah rubbed her cheek on her mother's leg. "Am I a Virgo kid?" she asked.

Her mother stroked her hair. "You're a Gemini. Niall, too. That's why you fight all the time."

Susannah pressed her lips together. She didn't want to tell her mother about her vow. Not yet.

"Hey," her mother said, "What's the matter?"

"Nothing," Susannah said. "I was thinking about astrology."

Her mother looked at her with an odd expression. Then she turned to glance through into the front hall. "Niall's being too quiet. You know where he is?"

Oh, who cares, Susannah thought. "He's playing with his horse."

"The new one? Good. Maybe he'll stay quiet for a while."

Hah, Susannah thought. Bet he won't.

Suddenly her mother put her hand on her belly. "*Woo.*"

"What?" Susannah said.

"The baby kicked!" Her mother beckoned. "Come up next to me." Susannah moved up to sit beside her mother. "Feel."

Susannah stretched out her hand. Her mother took it and guided it to a place on her belly. Susannah felt a sharp quiver against her palm.

"Feel that?"

"Uh huh." Susannah swallowed. "Does it hurt?"

"Nope."

"What does it feel like?"

Her mother laughed. "It feels like a burp."

"Oh." Suddenly Susannah felt it again. Like a baby chicken, she thought, pecking at a shell. That made her feel strange. Jerking her hand away, she rubbed it on her knee.

Her mother touched her cheek softly. "Hey, Susie-pooh," she said. "You know, there's a live person in there. Toes and ears and a heart and everything, almost ready to come out."

"I know that," Susannah said, annoyed. She had seen pictures and knew what babies looked like before they were born.

"Which would you prefer," her mother said, "a boy or a girl?"

I don't want it at all, Susannah thought. But she couldn't say that.

Babies were babies: they cried and were wet all the time. There was a baby on the street already: Juanito, Danielle's brother. She wondered if a little sister would be as much hassle as a brother. "I don't care."

"Mmm," said her mother. She stretched her arms above her head. "Are we out of milk?"

Susannah tried to picture the inside of the refrigerator as she had seen it last. "I don't remember."

"Would you look?"

7

"Okay." She went in. The house seemed very dark. The kitchen tile was cool on her bare feet. She opened the refrigerator.

There were usually two big gallon containers of milk on the middle shelf. There was one there now. She reached in and took it out. It was very light.

"Merow," said a voice near the ground. Something warm and soft and furry brushed her left leg.

"Hello, Mr. D," she said.

The big square orange cat butted his head on her knee. "Mowr," he said.

"I know what you want." Susannah took his water bowl from its place and put it on the kitchen table. Then she poured the rest of the milk—it was only a tiny bit—into the bowl. "Come on," she whispered.

Mr. D jumped to the table top. Purring, he folded himself up beside the bowl and drank. Susannah put the empty container in the pantry and went out. "There was a little left," she said. "I gave it to Mr. D."

"Dad can get more tomorrow. But we'll need some tonight. Would you go to the store and get a quart?" Mother dug into her pocket and brought out a dollar. "Bring me the change."

"All right," Susannah said. Putting the dollar into her own pocket, she started down the steps.

"Put something on your feet!"

Her thongs were in the front hall. Wriggling her toes into them, Susannah went down the steps. Her mother waved from the top.

Susannah loved her street. It was named Allan Street and it was only one block long. There were lots of streets like it in San Francisco. Her father—he was a city bus driver, and knew all about the streets—had showed her on the city map: there was Carl Street and Paul Street and Jessie Street and Edna Street. There was no street named Susannah. But there was no street named Niall, either!

Allan Street's tall wooden houses had curly decorations and

designs all over them. Some of the houses were painted neat colors: blue and bright yellow and gold. Some even had stained glass windows! At the bottom of the street sat a little store, a park, and a streetcar line beside the park. Susannah loved to watch the red and yellow streetcar stop at the bottom of the hill before the tunnel. It would sit humming as people got off and on, and then it would close its doors—thunk, thunk!—and come rattling and shaking up the slope. At night she would hear it between dreams, like the soft snore of the cat, and it made her feel good.

At the entrance to the store Susannah stopped, hoping to see a streetcar heading for the tunnel, but none appeared. She went into the store. The cooler was in the back. She took a quart of milk from it and brought it to Al at the counter.

"How ya doing?" said Al, punching the buttons on his machine.

"All right," Susannah said, giving him her dollar. She watched him count out coins. She had heard Celie say that Al was an Arab and it made her curious—when he got home, did he take off his shirt and put on a headdress and a long white robe?

"Need a bag?" he asked. He always asked Mother that, and she always answered, "Nope. Save a tree."

Susannah shook her head. Al leaned over the counter to give her the change. As she stuck it in her pocket she wished that she could spend it to buy beef jerky. She loved the salty taste, and it was neat to tear at the tough flat strip with her teeth and pretend to be an Indian or a pioneer.

As she left the store, the label on a bottle caught her eye. A white horse. It made her think of Niall. Stupid brat. She kicked at a tuft of grass.

"Susannah!"

Susannah looked up. "Hi!" she said. And grinned.

"Hi," said Danielle.

Susannah and Danielle were best friends. Everyone knew it: the kids at school, Al, Mr. Gonzalez, even Niall. Danielle lived in the grey house across the corner from the store. Her house was plainer than Susannah's house, which was painted red and brown, but it had three stained glass windows.

"You going to the store?" Susannah asked.

Danielle shook her head. "Saw you from the window. Came to find you. My mom's at your house."

"Okay." They walked to Susannah's house. Celie sat on the porch beside Susannah's mother. She held Juanito on her lap.

"Hi, Sukie," Celie said.

"Hi," Susannah said. Danielle's mother made her feel shy, because she was beautiful. She was brown, and her hair was in tight shiny black curls all over her head. Danielle had hair like that too. Susannah's hair was brown and stringy. Sometimes she was jealous of Danielle's sleek curls. But not often, because it made her stomach ache to feel bad about her best friend.

Susannah climbed the steps and handed her mother the change. "Thank you, honey," her mother said. "Would you put the milk in the refrigerator, please?" She said to Celie, "The doctor told me last week—"

Danielle leaped up the steps past the two women. "Come on," she said over her shoulder.

In the kitchen, Susannah scowled. "All they ever talk about is babies!"

"My mom's just had a baby and yours is having one," Danielle said. "They don't talk about them when they aren't having them."

Opening the refrigerator, Susannah put the milk on the shelf. "That's true." But I'm sick of babies! she thought. First there was Niall, and now there'll be a new one.

They walked to the bedroom. "What's the baby's name gonna be?" Danielle asked.

"I don't know. How about Leia?" Danielle really liked Princess Leia. She had seen *Star Wars* six times. That was almost as many times as Niall had seen *The Black Stallion*.

"Naw. How about Luke Skywalker?"

"What if it's a girl? You can't name a girl Luke."

"Lulu," said Danielle. "Lulu Skywalker."

That was lame. They both laughed.

Outside the bedroom door, Susannah put a hand up. "Wait." She pushed the door slowly. Niall wasn't there. "It's okay—" she started to say, and stopped.

A pile of her favorite books—*her* books!—lay on the floor, all jumbled and open.

"Niall!" Susannah spun. But of course he was gone, probably giggling to himself under Mother and Daddy's big bed. "That brat!" Susannah knelt. Gently she closed each book. Then she carried them to the bookshelf and put each in its proper place. "I'd like to—to—" She couldn't think of anything she could do that would be horrible enough. She couldn't even go find him and scream at him, because she had vowed not to.

"Hey," said Danielle. "What're you doing tonight?"

Susannah shrugged. "I don't know. Maybe I'll paint."

Danielle grew serious. "Could I see the pictures when you finish?"

Susannah liked showing Danielle her pictures. She never said stupid stuff like "Why is the sky purple?" and she always knew what the picture was a picture of, even if it didn't come out.

"I'll try to bring them over," Susannah promised. She smiled, thinking of the little cakes of paint, like eggs, inside the new paint box.

Jeanne Gomoll

Chapter Two

But the pictures wouldn't come, even with the new paint box open on the living room floor beside her, its colors glowing.

"Make a picture of the rainbow," Mother said, looking at the blank paper over Susannah's shoulder.

Susannah shook her head. Her mother loved rainbows. But it was silly to paint a rainbow; they were always the same, in the same colors.

Wriggling a little, she stared at the paper. Dinner was over, but the house still smelled wonderful; it smelled of tomato and ground beef and onions and the spices that Mother had put in the spaghetti sauce. But even the good smells and the warmth in her stomach—two things that usually made Susannah feel as if she could do anything—were not helping her paint.

The TV blared gunfire from her parents' bedroom. Niall was watching some stupid show. Susannah scowled. She wanted to stomp down the hall and turn it off. It was distracting.

"Would you be more comfortable at the kitchen table?" Mother said. She knew something was wrong and was trying to help.

"No." Susannah wriggled closer to the paper, careful not to jog the water glass with her elbow. Niall had already knocked it over—accidentally on purpose—on his way to the TV.

She wanted to draw a picture of the silver horse. It was hard to draw from memory.

"You could draw Mr. D. Or Daddy's bus," her mother said.

Susannah wanted to scream. Leave me alone! She gripped her paintbrush hard. Shapes and colors squirmed inside her head. She saw the silver horse alive, not a toy, trotting through the city streets in the moonlight. Around him the city's skyscrapers made a big steel fence.

"Damn," she said very softly. She wasn't supposed to say that word. She dipped the paintbrush in the silver paint. I can draw the silver horse, she thought, I *can!*

But the paint dripped from the brush, speckling the paper. Susannah sat up and crumpled the paper into a ball. Her stomach had started to ache.

"Nooo!" Niall screamed from the bedroom. Mother had turned the TV off. She wanted him to go to bed. He didn't want to go; he never wanted to go to sleep no matter how tired he was. He came into the living room, yellow hair flying. He was wearing his blue pajamas with the horses on them.

"I want to stay up and see Daddy!" he yelled.

"No," Mother said. "He's driving late shift tonight."

"But I want to!"

"You know," Mother said, "instead of arguing with me, you should be thinking about your horse."

"Why?" Niall said suspiciously.

"Have you given it a name yet?"

"No."

"You should."

"Why?"

"Because you have to give it the right name," Mother said. "If you give your toys the wrong name, they won't stay with you. They'll run away."

"Where?" Niall asked.

"To the Land of Runaway Toys," Mother said solemnly.

"Where is that?" Niall asked. "Is it near Dreamland?"

Dreamland was a place that Mother had told Susannah and Niall about. It was a magic place, a part of Storyland. Storyland, Mother said, was where all the stories ever told in the whole world came true. Susannah knew it was a made-up place but she enjoyed thinking about it anyway. Sometimes she pretended it was real.

Someday, she thought, I'll draw a map of those places. Dreamland. Storyland. She would save a little corner of Storyland for the Land of Runaway Toys. She had seen such maps in books. Her favorites were the ones that left blank spaces in the oceans or the woods, and labelled them "Monsters," or "Here Be Tygers."

A picture slithered into her head. She saw the silver horse flying in the air. The ground beneath him was all wrinkly and squeezed together, like on some maps.

That's ridiculous, she thought. The silver horse can't fly. He has no wings!

But the picture was there. And it was a much better picture than anything she could draw. Susannah's stomach hurt so much, it felt as if she'd eaten rocks for dinner.

"Don't get discouraged," Mother said from the doorway. "It'll come."

No it won't, Susannah thought rebelliously. Nothing could come here. It's too noisy. People won't even let you alone to think!

She stood up. "Can I go out?"

"You want to go to Danielle's? Okay. But be back by nine o'clock."

"There's no school tomorrow," Susannah protested.

"Never mind. Just be here by nine."

"Okay." Susannah scooped her book and paint box from the floor. Going to the kitchen, she put the book and box on the table, knowing that her mother would put them in the bedroom. Her jacket was in the hall closet. She put it on. It was blue, with a rainbow on the back. Mother had bought it for her.

From the top step of her house she could see the entire street. At one end the red stop sign glowed beneath a streetlight. At the other, the red neon sign outside of Al's market blinked off and on. The stars were bright as dimes. The great white face of the full moon stared over the roofs of the houses across the street.

Susannah walked down the steps to the sidewalk. The houses looked smug, as if they were keeping secrets from the peering moon.

The moon seemed to watch her all the way to the end of the block.

She went up the steps to Danny's house and knocked. Celie opened the door. She was wearing a neat shirt; it was purple, and glittery. "Hi, Sukie. Danielle's in her room."

"Thank you." Susannah went to Danielle's bedroom. It was a smaller room than Susannah and Niall's room, but it was all Danielle's. Juanito slept in Celie's bedroom, in a crib.

Danny was sitting on her bed, staring down at a huge book. "Boo," Susannah said.

Danielle looked up. Her wide grin flashed. "Hi. Did you bring any pictures?"

Susannah scowled. "I couldn't make any tonight."

Danielle eyed her a moment, and then moved over to make room for her on the bed. "C'mere." She patted the bed. Susannah climbed up beside her.

Danny leaned across the bulk of the book to hug her. "Never mind," she said. Her breath was warm on Susannah's ear. "Never mind. You will."

Her arms were wiry and strong. Susannah felt the aching knot in her stomach begin to loosen. "What're you looking at?" she said.

Danielle thumped the book. "This. See this?" *This* was a photograph of a mountain with snow on top. The mountain looked very high, and very cold. "Its name is Mount Rainier. It's in Washington. I'm going to climb it."

Danielle loved mountains the way Niall loved horses. She had pictures of them all over her wall and even in the bathroom so she could look at them when she brushed her teeth. She wanted to be a fire ranger and live on top of one.

"*What's* it called?"

"Rainier."

"What's that mean?"

"I don't know. Maybe it rains a lot there."

Susannah nodded. That made sense. She leaned against the wall. Danny's room was warm and it smelled like Danny. "I was trying to draw a picture of Niall's horse," she explained. "But it was really hard."

"Harder than the cat?"

"Oh yeah!" Susannah said. "Much harder."

"It is a neat horse," Danny agreed. "Mom was gonna paint it gold. But I think silver turned out better, don't you?"

Susannah tried to picture the horse painted gold. "Ugh. Gold would look too plastic." She recalled her vision of the silver horse flying over a map. There was a winged horse in a story—the same

16

story that had the lady whose hair was snakes. Susannah tried to remember the horse's name, and couldn't.

"What if you had to give the horse a name?" she asked. "What would you call it?"

Danny frowned. "Name it? Why name it? It's a toy."

"My mother told Niall about a place toys run to if you don't give them the right name."

Danielle was frequently scornful of Bonnie's stories, but this time her dark face grew thoughtful. "Toys do disappear. Remember my old wooden train?" Susannah nodded. It had been made of dust-colored blocks with painted wheels. "I wanted it one day and I couldn't find it. I never gave it a name; it was only a train. You think it ran away?"

Susannah spread her hands. "It's just a story."

"Huh." Danny opened the book. "You like weird names? There's a neat one here." She lugged the book over to Susannah's lap and leafed through it. "There! This is the tallest mountain in the world. It has two names: Mount Everest and Cho-mo-lung-ma. That's its real name. It means Goddess Mother of the World. Isn't that boss?"

Susannah gazed at the pictures of Chomolungma. She wondered why the sky around the snow-capped peak looked black. Maybe the pictures had been taken at night. How tall was the tallest mountain in the world? Could you stand on top of it? If you stood on top of it, would you see San Francisco?

"Where'd you get the book?"

"From my Aunt Marie," Danielle said. Danny's aunt worked downtown at the big library. She knew about interesting books before anyone else did. "The library was selling it, because it's old and gross." She closed the book. Its front cover was scratched.

"So what?" Susannah said. "The pages aren't torn."

They started to look at the pictures, but got stuck in the middle of the book and never made it to the end. Danielle read bits of it aloud. She read about Sherpas. Sherpas lived in the mountains and climbed up and down them all the time. "If I can't be a ranger," Danny said, "I'll be a Sherpa."

"I think it's like being an American or a Californian," Susannah said. "You have to be born there."

"No," Danny said, "I looked it up in the encyclopedia. There's no place named Sherp."

Finally Celie stuck her head around the door. "Sukie, what time you supposed to be home?"

"Nine o'clock."

"It's nine-fifteen."

"Whoops!" Susannah leaped off the bed. Grabbing her jacket from the floor where she had dumped it, she whirled to hug Danielle. "Bye! See you tomorrow."

She raced up the street to her house. The moon, high overhead, was bright as the street lamps. Wisps of fog were blowing from the west.

She pounded up the stairs. Her mother was waiting for her. "I was just going to call," she murmured, lifting the jacket from Susannah's shoulders.

Her bed was waiting. The covers were turned back. Niall was asleep already, his hair spread like gold threads over the pillow. He hugged his old stuffed horse Windy in his arms.

The new horse stood on the lid of the toy chest. Beside it, was Mr. D. His eyes were huge.

"What have you been saying to each other?" Susannah said, peeling off her pants.

Mr. D stretched, poking his rump high in the air. Susannah went to him and stroked him. The silver horse seemed to watch her. Impulsively, Susannah reached out and touched its back. Under the texture of the paint, the wood was smooth and warm.

As soon as she got into bed, Mr. D jumped on to the foot of the bed and curled into a ball. His eyes made slits. D is for diamond, Susannah thought. But all cats have diamond eyes.

Mother came in. Bending, she tucked the covers around

Susannah's shoulders. She clicked the light off. "Sleep time. Go to Dreamland, Susie-pooh."

Susannah yawned, and stretched her toes against the cat. Near the floor the night-light glowed. It was shaped like a smiling pumpkin.

"Mother?"

"Mmm?"

Susannah turned her head so that she could see her mother's face. "What will you and Daddy name the new baby?"

Her mother smiled. "If it's a boy, David. If it's a girl, Corinna."

"Corinna's a pretty name."

"No prettier than Susannah."

"No," Susannah agreed. She was feeling sleepy. Mr. D. at her feet was purring and purring, vibrating into her toes and up her legs and along her arms and all the way to her eyelids. "If you gave the baby the wrong name, would it run away like the toys?"

"No," her mother said. "People don't run away for those reasons."

"Why do they?"

"Run away? Because they're unhappy where they are."

"Oh," Susannah said. She yawned. "It might be fun to visit."

"The Land of Runaway Toys? Go to sleep, and maybe you'll dream about it." She kissed Susannah's cheek. "Remember, Susie–only–pooh, it's just a story."

Stories are real, too, Susannah thought, only they happen in your head. A streetcar rumbled toward the park. I'll stay awake until the next one, she decided. Just until the next streetcar goes by . . .

A sparkle woke her.

Susannah stared at the ceiling. She blinked. The room was bright. Turning from her stomach on to her side, she saw why: the shade over the window had rolled up. Moonlight poured through the window.

Susannah rubbed her eyes, feeling with her toes for the comfortable bulk of Mr. D at the foot of the bed. He wasn't there. She lifted on her elbows to look at the door. It was open, and Niall's bed was empty. The moonlight was so intense it made her eyes sting. Susannah put her arm over her face. Niall must have gone to the bathroom, she thought.

Suddenly she heard him whispering. "Horse, wait for me."

A cold finger tickled Susannah's spine. Shuddering, she sat upright. The room was so bright she could barely see the face of the night light.

"Horse, wait!"

Susannah gazed at the squat shape of the toy chest. The silver horse was not where it should be, poised and still in the light. What was Niall doing? She pictured him in his blue pajamas with the horses on them, playing some private moonstruck game up and down the hallway. Stupid brat. She pushed the covers aside. The floor was cold. She yawned. Perhaps she could coax Niall back to bed before he woke Daddy.

She could let him wake Daddy, and get smacked.

Then she heard, from the other end of the house, a beat of sound. It was the front door closing.

Susannah almost wailed aloud. Then she scrambled for her shirt and jeans and socks and tennis shoes. *I'll* smack him, she thought with fervor and fury. He's taken that horse and gone to play in the park!

She wondered as she tied her shoelaces if she should wake her father. She wasn't supposed to go to the park either, after dark. But it was so bright, almost like daylight, and her legs were longer than his . . . She would catch him before he got there. Holding her breath, Susannah crept down the hall past her parents' bedroom. The front door was ajar. Quietly she pushed the button to unlock the door so that she and Niall could get back in. Then, heart beating hard, she left the house.

The moon was so bright that the lamp posts and telephone poles all had double shadows. The wind snapped at her with foggy teeth. Should have brought my jacket, she thought, hugging her shirt to her sides. Stubborn and shivering she ran, peering ahead for a yellow-haired boy wearing blue pajamas and carrying a glitter-flecked horse.

He was too far away; she could not see him. He had gotten away from her. Fists clenched, she stopped at the street to look both ways. The moon flung her shadow ahead of her as she ran across the silver streetcar rails to the park.

The grass was wet; Susannah felt it on her ankles through her socks. "Niall!" she called. Her voice seemed lost. The park, not large in the daytime, seemed to stretch for miles. Deep shadows crouched beneath the trees.

"Niall!" she shouted. "Niall, come here, it's me. It's Susannah!"

From somewhere, like an echo, her name came back to her. "Susannah!"

She turned in a circle. The fog was so thick that she could not see her own house. Suddenly she saw Niall. He stood in the middle of the park. Behind him, like a dream come to life, was the silver horse, gleaming in the moonlight and *growing* as it glowed. Shivering, Susannah rubbed her eyes. The horse was still there. It cantered across the grass in a great circle around Niall. Its hooves, Susannah saw with wonder, were inches from the ground.

"Horse!" called Niall. He flung his arms up.

"Niall!" Susannah yelled. She ran toward him.

"Susannah!" someone called.

The horse neighed. It was a strong, clear, beautiful sound. It bent its head to let Niall clasp its mane. He scrambled to its back. He looked very small in the swirling fog. Susannah stood openmouthed.

This is a dream, she thought desperately. She pinched herself hard on one arm.

Go back, said a voice in her head, go back, go home, wake your parents. "Niall!" she called. He didn't look at her. But the horse looked straight at her. Its eyes were red, like rubies. It neighed again, and began to climb. As if it were on solid ground, it stepped into the creeping fog, and the fog bore it up. Higher and higher it pranced, until it was above the street lights. The moon blazed through the fog like a beacon.

A woman's voice called sweetly through the darkness. "Come," she called. Her voice was clear and compelling. The horse reared, and leaped at the glowing moon. Susannah saw it silhouetted against the light. Niall was a small lump on its back.

Then it was gone.

The fog writhed over the shadowy grass. The moon sailed serenely through the sky. Susannah, heart pounding in her chest, ran over the wet grass to where the horse had been.

As she reached the spot, the world turned upside down. The fog enveloped her. Her feet left the ground. Her stomach lurched as she saw below her the fog, the park, the street, her house, small, and getting smaller.

The moon filled her vision. A flash of cold fire broke over her head like a wave, and she was falling—falling—it seemed a long way down.

Jeanne Gomoll

Chapter Three

Susannah woke.

Her head felt fuzzy. There was a lovely smell in the air, a smell like flowers and honey and music. Mr. D was purring beside her. Okay, cat, she thought, time to get up now.

She stretched and rolled over. Something hard and unexpected poked her in the back. "Ow!" she said indignantly. Then she really woke, and opened her eyes.

Above her was the sky, patched with pieces of green.

She sat up. Grass prickled on her palms. She remembered: she had chased Niall into the park. The silver horse had grown big and jumped into the moon. And then—and then she had fallen somewhere. Here. Here was gray: a pearly clear gray, not a foggy San Francisco gray. She lay under the branches of a tree. Mr. D, sun-colored, sat at her feet washing his ears, imperturbable as only a cat can be about anything.

Was she in the park? Susannah looked for a playground, the swings, the green benches. But there was only grass—more grass than she had ever seen, a sweet-smelling, luxurious lawn—and a big green tree, and a small brown-haired girl, and a ginger cat.

She was not in the park.

"I'm dreaming," Susannah said aloud to the still morning.

She wondered where she was. There didn't seem to be anything happening. She hoped her mother and father had not awakened and followed her to the park. She pictured them wandering through the thick fog, hunting through the bushes, calling "Niall! Susannah!"

Mr. D yawned, snapping his jaws together with mock energy. He seemed unconcerned about the disappearance of his house. Susannah scrambled to her feet. She wasn't scared, she thought, brushing her jeans free of loose dirt. There was nothing scary about grass and a tree. If she was dreaming then there was nothing to be afraid of; dreams never hurt you, and eventually you woke up. If she was not dreaming then she was having an Adventure.

"How did *you* get here?" she asked the cat. "Did you follow me to the park, and jump into the moon?"

Mr. D switched his tail.

"I didn't see you."

Switch, switch.

"Do you think we're in Storyland?"

25

Switch.

"Do you think Niall's here too?"

He yawned.

"Well, I don't speak Cat," Susannah said. She squinted. "I see a rock," she told Mr. D. "A big brown rock."

He wasn't interested. We have rocks at home, he seemed to be saying.

Susannah gazed at the tree. It was really huge. The trunk was smooth and gray, with red lines running through the bark. She wondered what kind of tree it was and if something lived inside it— an elf, a dwarf, a squirrel?

"This is a weird place," she said to the cat, "with only a rock and a tree in it. There must be people somewhere." She combed her hair with her fingers and started to walk. She walked around the tree. It looked the same no matter which side of it she was on.

Finally, because it was something to do, she started to walk to the rock. "Come on, Mr. D," she said. She hoped he would follow her; even though she wasn't scared, it seemed pleasant to have Mr. D. nearby, big and furry and unchanged.

Maybe he wouldn't want to be alone in this strange place either. She looked back. The cat hadn't moved. "Mr. D?"

The cat looked at her, licked his left paw, stretched, and strolled toward her.

Susannah walked and walked. Then she walked some more. When she looked back she could see the track she had left in the grass, all the way to the tree. The tree looked small now. To her left the sky was growing brighter, turning from gray to a soft pale blue. Far away on the horizon stretched a line of gold. It was warm and very still. There were no cars, no streetcars, no people clomping to work, not even any birds. The loudest sound was the rustling in the grass of Susannah's own strides, going *Shhh*.

What if she had come to a part of Storyland where there were no people at all?

There had to be people somewhere. Susannah swallowed, and rubbed her arms with her hands. Her knees felt shaky. Adventures always had people in them. Who else would the stories happen to?

When she reached the rock, she would climb on it and look around. There would be people somewhere.

But the rock was very far away. By the time she reached it she was hot and thirsty, and her legs hurt, and her stomach was starting to growl. It didn't look like an easy rock to climb, either, Susannah thought as she surveyed it. It was taller than she was, and very smooth, not rough and bumpy the way rocks were supposed to be, and there was stuff growing on it, all over it, stuff like short brown grass. . . .

Suddenly she jumped back. The rock was *moving*.

It was standing up.

It was turning around. It *looked* at her.

It wasn't a rock.

It was an immense brown furry bear.

Susannah froze, too frightened to run or scream. She stared upward. The bear didn't growl or snarl or anything, it simply towered over her, blinking. Then it yawned. It had more teeth than she had ever seen in her life, and when its jaws shut, she heard an echo.

"Hello," it said.

Susannah jumped. "Hello."

"How did you get here?" it asked. It had a deep rumbly voice.

Susannah swallowed. "I just woke up under the tree."

"Ah." It liked that sound. It rocked back and forth on its huge feet, nodding, and said it several times. "Ah. Ah. You're a child, aren't you?"

"Yes." Would it eat her now? Did bears eat people? She had never heard of bears eating people—at least, not talking bears.

"That's odd, that's very odd," it said. "Children don't come here." Lines appeared on its forehead. It seemed to be thinking. "Unless—were you looking for someone?"

27

Was she looking for someone? Susannah wasn't sure. Then she remembered the silver horse and Niall. Niall! Stupid brat. "Yes," she said, "I am looking for someone. I guess I am. Why? Have you seen anyone?"

The bear shook its great head. "No," it said. It gazed at her mournfully. "I'm sorry."

"That's all right," Susannah said. There didn't seem to be anything else to say. She glanced at Mr. D, wondering if he was going to start to talk, too, but he was busy examining a grass blade.

The bear cleared its throat. "I suppose, if you just woke up, that you'd like breakfast?"

Susannah's stomach fizzed wildly. "Yes!" she said. Then she thought, What do bears like for breakfast?

"So would I," said the bear. "Would you like to ride?" Reaching up, it patted an ample shoulder. "It's pretty far away."

Susannah didn't know what to do. What if breakfast meant *her*? It would be difficult to run away from a hungry bear if you were riding on its shoulders. But this bear had a kind voice. It didn't sound as if it wanted to eat her.

"Okay," she said.

The bear bent and picked her up gently, in its two soft brown paws. Grass and sky swung. Then she was set firmly on the bear's broad shoulders. "You can hold my fur," said the bear.

In the grass, Mr. D was a small orange lump. Susannah clutched the bear's fur with both hands. "Where are we going?"

The bear dropped slowly from its hind legs to all fours and began to move through the grass. "To the banana tree," it answered.

The bear traveled slowly. Every now and then it stopped, swaying from side to side, to say hello to the flowers that had begun to appear. Mr. D wound about the huge brown feet, clearly unafraid of the big shuffling beast.

Soon Susannah saw a smudge of color on the horizon. The smudge grew closer, larger. . . . Susannah gaped. The bear trotted into a jungle of trees and vines and scarlet flowers. A long green vine looped near her face. Colorful butterflies swooped around her head. Flowers thrust their petals at her eyes. Around her the chatter of birds echoed, deafening after the cool silence of the grasslands.

"The banana tree's over there," rumbled the bear.

Susannah had seen palm trees, but she had never seen a banana tree. It was very tall and so broad that she couldn't see around it. Yellow bananas and green bananas and shriveled black bananas hung from it in bunches. Reaching out, the bear picked two yellow bananas off a bunch. It handed one to Susannah.

"Thank you," she said.

"You're welcome." It peeled the banana rather messily with its teeth. Susannah wondered why it didn't use its claws. She looked at its paws.

It didn't have any claws.

That made her feel better. Peeling her own banana, she hung the skin on a branch, wondering what her mother would say about a banana for breakfast.

"Want another?" said the bear.

"I'll split it with you," Susannah said.

So they each ate half a banana, and the bear had another whole one and then a third whole one. Susannah wondered what her mother would say about *three* bananas for breakfast.

Whoop! *Whoop!* Whoopwhoopwhoopwhoopwhoop! A horrible siren screamed at them through the jungle. Susannah looked around, wondering what could be making the awful sound.

"What is it?" she said. The bear didn't answer; it simply waved one paw in the air helplessly.

WHOOPWHOOPWHOOP! The birds all flew out of the surrounding trees.

Could it be a police car? Susannah thought. Were they going to be arrested for stealing bananas?

But no police car butted its way through the vines, to foul the air with smoke and crush the beautiful jungle flowers. Instead, the banana tree shook, and a black and white face peered at them from between two bunches of bananas.

"That's three, that's three, that's three!" it said.

The bear hung its head. "Oh, all right." It sounded embarrassed.

"You're going to get fat, fat, fat!"

Oh, Susannah thought. It's a *monkey*.

The monkey had a black face with a white band across its forehead, and extremely long arms. It was gripping a branch of the banana tree with one of them. It waved the other in Susannah's face. "Who's this, this, this?"

The bear said, "Uh—"

"My name's Susannah," said Susannah.

"Susannah, Susannah, Susannah," said the monkey. It liked saying things three times.

Susannah wondered why it didn't introduce itself. "Who are you?" she said at last.

"This is Chimp," the bear said.

"WHOOP! WHOOP! WHOOP!" The noise echoed through the jungle. The agitated monkey leaped up and down, screaming like a demented fire engine.

"My name is not Chimp," it said. "Chimp is for chimpanzee—zee—zee and I am not a chimpanzee. I am a gibbon, and I make more noise than anybody!" The ape took off like a rocket, leaping from tree to tree in a dizzying circle around the girl and the bear, shrieking.

When at last it sat still on a branch, Susannah took her hands from her ears and said, "What *is* your name?"

"Aloysius," the gibbon said. "Chimp!" it repeated with extreme scorn. "That's what the child who bought me thought. He called me Chimp. I ran away that very night!"

"Oh!" said Susannah.

"Oh, oh, oh," the gibbon chattered, mocking her. "Oh, what?"

"This must be the Land of Runaway Toys."

"You didn't know?" the bear rumbled, surprised.

Susannah shook her head. She hadn't expected it to look like this. She gazed with admiration at the iridescent jungle.

Suddenly she knew why the bear had a shiny nose like a button and soft paws with no claws. "You're a Teddy Bear!" she said.

"Yes." The bear sighed. "I am."

Susannah was no longer afraid of the bear at all. She stroked his soft fur. "How did you get so big?"

The bear rubbed its shiny nose with one paw. "I'm a *grown-up* teddy bear." The gibbon made a chuckling noise. It sounded like a nutcracker. "I wasn't always this big. When I was very, very small, a little girl brought me home from the toy store. She had black hair tied in blue ribbons; I remember very clearly."

"But why are you here?"

The bear scuffed its big feet in the dirt. "I ran away," it said. "She kept calling me 'Teddy.'"

"Teddy," gibed the gibbon, "Teddy, Teddy."

Susannah scowled at the gibbon. Really, she thought, how rude. "Please go on," she said to the bear.

"All my brothers and sisters are named Teddy," the bear explained, "but I was the youngest, you see, and Mother decided she wanted to name me something different."

"What did she name you?"

Sadly the bear shook its head from side to side. "Murgatroyd."

"Murgatroyd!" Aloysius screamed, "Murgatroyd, Murgatroyd!"

"You shut up," Susannah said to the gibbon. "Is that so terrible?" she said to the bear.

"Well, it isn't exactly a common name."

"No," Susannah agreed. The bear looked so depressed at that that she added, "But it's a more *interesting* name than Teddy."

"Do you really think so?" said the bear. Susannah nodded emphatically. "Thank you. It's kind of you to say so. Everyone else thinks it's funny." It rubbed its nose again. "I liked it here at first.

It was fun, getting big. But now I'm all alone, the only bear in the Land of Runaway Toys. There's nobody here to play with me."

"That's the saddest thing I ever heard," Susannah said. "Why won't they play with you?"

"I'm too big."

"But aren't there other big animals here?" Susannah said. "Like—like elephants?"

"Yes," said the bear. "But elephants are always so serious, you know. They aren't interested in playing. I get lonely."

Susannah knew just what the bear meant. No place would feel strange if you had a friend along. As she thought it, she found herself wishing for a friend to share this Adventure with. Mr. D was there—but after all, Mr. D was only a cat. And Murgatroyd, though nice, was only a toy bear, and Aloysius was a noisy, nosy monkey.

Her nose began to itch alarmingly. Susannah rubbed it hard. I wish Danny were here with me, she thought. Or even Niall . . . She wondered where Niall was. Maybe, she thought, he was alone too. He was only six. Stupid brat. Probably he was frightened.

"Are there any children here?" she asked. "Or are there only toys?"

"I've never seen a child here, except for you," the bear answered.

But the gibbon said, "I saw a child last night."

"What?"

"I saw, I saw, I saw a child! Riding the Silver Horse. They went to the Lady's Hill."

"A child on a horse? Was it a boy in blue pajamas, with yellow hair like a dandelion?"

"Its hair was yellow," said the gibbon, "but I don't know if it was a boy. What's the difference?"

"Never mind," Susannah said. "Was he small? Smaller than me? Dressed in blue?"

"Yes, yes, yes."

It was Niall! Susannah looked around, half-hoping to see her brother step yawning out from amid the flowers. "Where did he go?" she asked.

"I told you," the gibbon said. "The Horse went to the Lady's Hill."

"What's that? How do I get there?"

"Don't know, don't know, don't know," chanted the gibbon.

Susannah decided that she didn't like the gibbon very much. "Who knows? Do you?" she asked the bear.

It shook its head from side to side.

"The Old Woman knows," the gibbon said abruptly.

"The Old Woman? Who's she?"

"She is," said the gibbon.

"How do I find her?" Susannah almost shouted. She was getting very impatient with asking questions.

The bear answered. "You can go through the jungle—" it pointed—"into the woods. She lives in the woods. She can tell you how to get to the Hill."

Through the jungle, and into a woods. Susannah wondered how long that would take. "What's the Old Woman like?" she asked. "Is she mean?"

Both animals gazed at her blankly. The bear had to twist its head all the way around on its shoulders.

Susannah frowned. "Put me down."

Murgatroyd reached up with its big soft paws and swung her to the earth. It looked sad. "I thought maybe you would stay and play with me."

"I'm sorry, Murgatroyd," Susannah said. "I'd like to. But I have to find my brother. He's younger than I am, and he's all alone. He might be frightened. You could come with me."

"I don't go into the woods." The bear sounded as if it wanted to cry.

"Don't sound so sad," Susannah begged. "I'll come back."

The bear sniffed, and wiped its nose with the back of its paw. It was clear that it didn't believe her.

"Which way do I go to get to the woods?" Susannah said. The jungle seemed very large now that she was not seated on the bear's shoulders. She could just make out the gibbon's black and white face hidden among the leaves of the banana tree.

The bear pointed. "That way. There's a trail."

Good, Susannah thought.

"Hey," said the gibbon. It swung down through the leaves until it was hanging from the lowest branch of the gigantic tree. Susannah noticed that it had no tail. "A word of warning," it said. "Don't fall asleep in the woods. It's dangerous."

"*What's* dangerous?" Susannah said.

The exasperating animal only shook its head. "Don't know, don't know, don't know. Don't go, don't go!"

"I have to!" Susannah said. "I have to find my brother." She looked around for Mr. D. He had vanished. Probably the gibbon's howls had scared him, or else he had gone to chase butterflies. There were a lot of butterflies in the jungle. Susannah wasn't worried about him; cats, unlike people, were always having Adventures. But she didn't really want to travel through a dangerous woods alone.

She stuck her chin out and thrust her hands in her pockets, trying to feel brave. "Good-bye," she said to the gibbon. "Good-bye, Murgatroyd. Thank you for breakfast."

"Good-bye," said the bear. It leaned down close to her. Its breath warmed her face. It whispered in her ear, "*You* can call me Mug."

Susannah was touched. Reaching out, she stroked the bear's forehead. "Thank you," she said, and added, whispering so that the nosy, nasty gibbon dangling nearby would not hear her, "Good-bye, Mug."

Jeanne Gomoll

Chapter Four

The woods were very dark.

The jungle had been dark, too: a lush, wet darkness, filled with movement and sound. The woods were quiet, like the grasslands. Almost quiet. As she walked, Susannah could hear the branches of the tall pine trees rubbing against one another in the wind. There were no birds calling, no insects or animals scurrying around on the forest floor. The dry creak of branches and the soft crunch of pine needles under Susannah's feet were the only sounds.

That's how trees in Storyland talk to one another. They rub their branches together, like crickets' legs. Susannah tipped her head back. The thick green-needled trees towered above her, shutting out the sun. Their size made her feel very small. More than ever she wished she had a friend beside her.

"Heh-heh-heh."

The odd sound seemed to emerge from the air. Susannah turned in a circle, trying to see what made the noise. It sounded like old, dry voices, laughing.

"Heh-heh-heh."

There it was again. Susannah scowled. I wouldn't live in this forest, she thought. It's creepy in here. She wondered why the Old Woman chose to live in such an unpleasant place, and if that meant that *she* was unpleasant.

Suddenly she leaped back. She had walked past a big knothole in one of the trees and a little man had thrust his head out and made a face at her!

She stared at the knothole. It was empty. Dumbhead, she told herself. You saw a squirrel. She walked around the tree and back to the trail. It's this creepy place, she decided; it makes me think I'm seeing things.

But she hadn't seen any squirrels.

Then she heard the voice.

"Help!" It was hard to hear. "Help!" The dark trees leaned together as if they wanted to shut out the sound. Beneath Susannah's feet the pine needles creaked their ugly laughter.

"Hello?"

"Hello," came the call back.

Susannah scowled. It's not a real voice. It's a trick to keep me from finding the Old Woman. It sounds familiar. Maybe it's an echo.

"Hello? Is someone there?" the voice called.

Susannah swallowed. I guess it isn't an echo. "Where are you?" she yelled.

"Here!" said the voice.

"Keep yelling!" Susannah cried. She ran toward the sound. Her feet made long gouges in the pine needle carpet.

"Here!" The voice was much closer now. It sounded like—it sounded— "Here! Here!"

She was there. So was Danielle.

Danny was wearing her faded blue jeans with the yellow patch on the knee and a red pajama top over them. She was sitting on the ground with her back against a tall pine tree.

"What are you doing here?" Susannah said. She wondered through her surge of joy why Danielle didn't get up to hug her.

Then she saw. Danielle couldn't get up. She was tied to the tree by two ropes. One went around her chest and arms. A second circled her waist. The ropes had red and blue stripes on them. They were, Susannah realized with a shiver, jump ropes.

"Danny! What happened?"

And around them both rose a hundred creaky voices. "Heh-heh-heh," they said, with nasty delight.

Danny said grimly, "They happened."

Susannah whirled.

They were dolls. There were a lot of them: tiny dolls, big dolls, pink and brown and patchwork dolls, Barbie dolls and Raggedy Anns. Some had one arm, some one leg, some no eyes, all were dirty, bruised, broken. . . .

Of course, Susannah realized, as they shuffled forward, glaring malignantly at her, that's what they all are. They're broken dolls.

"Susannah!" Danny said. "Don't back up."

Susannah gulped. She had been edging backward. The broken dolls, she saw, were carrying more jump ropes. Her heart began to beat very fast. If they grabbed her—and there *were* a lot of them—

they could hold her down and tie her and she and Danielle would sit forever in this horrible creepy place. . . . Not forever. Just until the Adventure ends. Adventures are like dreams. You never get hurt in dreams.

The doll closest to her had one arm, one leg, and no eyes in his eye sockets. A rubber band dangled from his exposed shoulder joint. Some child did that, Susannah thought. How mean. Feeling sorry for him, she held her hand out, trying to be friendly.

"We haven't hurt you," she said. "Please go away."

Danny said, "That won't work. I tried."

The dolls grinned at her. They scrambled forward dragging their ropes, creaking at her with their horrible malevolent laughter.

"Stop!" Susannah shouted.

They stopped and swayed back slightly, away from her.

"Maybe you could throw something at them," Danny said.

Susannah looked for a stick or a rock to throw. There were only pine needles on the ground. "There's nothing to throw!"

The dolls inched closer.

The eyeless doll had brown clumps of wool on top of his head. Some child had pulled the rest out. Through her fear Susannah could not help wondering how he and the other dolls without eyes saw.

"Heh-heh-heh," said the doll with no eyes, hopping nearer.

He waved the jump rope. Suddenly Susannah was not scared, but angry. It came up from her middle like a huge wave. She wanted to hit; she felt hot all over. Glaring at the dolls, she said, "You can't touch me! I'll knock you down. I'll pull all your hair out and pull off your legs. I'll kick you. I'll rub your faces in the dirt. I'll—" but she didn't have to say any more. Quick as squirrels in the trees, the broken dolls were gone.

"Whooee!" yelled Danielle.

Susannah took a deep breath. She felt limp all over.

"Girl, don't just stand there. Come and get me loose!"

Kneeling in the pine needles, Susannah prodded the knots that

held Danielle tied. She picked at them with her fingernails. "They're real tight. Maybe I could bite them—"

"You don't have to bite them," Danny said. "My pocket knife's in my left front pocket."

Wriggling her hand into the left front pocket of Danny's jeans, Susannah yanked it inside out. Everything fell in a pile on the ground. She sorted through the pile: in it were four pieces of string, some dirty tissues, a fragment of a sand dollar, a mashed snail shell without the snail, the cap off a blue pen, and a very small pocket knife with two blades.

Susannah pulled one of the blades out.

"That's the nail file," Danny said. "It's the other one."

The blade took a long time to cut the ropes. "You keep watch," Susannah said. "They might come back."

"Right," said Danny.

At last both ropes lay parted on the ground. Rubbing her arms, Danielle pushed away from the tree. She flung her arms apart. They hugged. "I'm really glad to see you!" Danny said.

"Me too," Susannah said. "How did you get here?"

"I followed you," Danny said. She brushed the pine needles from her jeans. "Didn't you hear me calling? I was at my window, watching the moonlight, when I saw Niall running down the street and then you. I sneaked out the back door and climbed over the fence just as you went into the park."

Danielle climbed fences very quickly. "I did hear you," Susannah said. "I heard you call my name."

"Why didn't you wait?"

"I didn't know it was you. And I was trying to catch Niall. Did you see—" Susannah hesitated. "Did you see what happened?"

Danny's dark face was solemn. "I saw the horse get big and jump into the moon. I thought I was dreaming. Then the fog wrapped itself around me and wouldn't let go." She picked up the string and the sand dollar and the pen cap and the pocket knife.

"I'm glad you're here," Susannah said. "I was lonely."

Then she saw the tears running down Danny's face.

"Hey," she said. She put an arm around Danielle. "Hey. Sit down." She wanted to sit and put her arms all the way around Danielle and rock her, the way Mother did when *she* cried. But Danny stiffened her shoulders and shook her head. She kept making faces to keep from crying, but it didn't help. The tears kept rolling down her cheeks.

Finally the tears ran out. "I deed to blow by dose," Danny said.

"Here," said Susannah, remembering the tissues. They were still lying in the pine needles. With careful unfolding, Danielle found a corner she could use.

"You okay?" Susannah said.

"Yeah." Danielle rubbed her sleeve across her face. She tossed the tissues to the ground. "It was so dark in here, you know. When the fog grabbed me I jumped, or fell. I'm not sure which. I landed here. I stayed awake for a long time. Then I fell asleep. When I woke up, those little monsters were all over me."

Susannah shuddered. The forest was scary in daylight. It must have been horrible at night. "I'd've been really scared."

"I was," Danny said. She tucked her pajama top inside her belt. "They looked like dolls, you know?"

"They are dolls," Susannah said. "This is the Land of Runaway Toys."

Danny frowned. "But I thought—"

"What?"

"I thought that was just a story." She stood still, looking at the trees. "Is that where we are? In a story?"

"I think so," Susannah said.

"Oh. Do you know how to get out of here?"

"There's a trail."

They hunted through the trees until they found the trail.

"Which way?" said Danny.

Susannah wasn't sure. "Wait," she said. She walked along it until she came to a place where the pine needles were scattered.

"This way," she said, pointing to the undisturbed length of trail. "Those are the marks I made when I started to run."

They walked.

"Where are we going?" Danny said. "I'm just following you."

"To find an old woman who lives in the woods."

"In here?" Danny stopped short. "I don't want to stay here. I hate this place, it stinks. I want to go home."

"Me too!" Susannah said. "But I have to find Niall. He's here. What if someone's grabbed him and tied him up? He's only a little kid. Anyway, I don't know yet how to get home."

"Oh," Danny said. Her face twisted.

"There'll be a way," Susannah said quickly. "There always is, in stories."

"Huh." Danny sniffed. She kicked the ground. "Baby brothers are the pits, aren't they? They always do stupid stuff and get into trouble."

"Yeah."

"Does this old lady know where Niall is?"

"I hope so," Susannah said. "The gibbon said she would."

"The what?"

Susannah told Danny about Murgatroyd and Aloysius.

"Wow," said Danny. "You making this up?"

"No!"

"A talking teddy bear? Huh. Niall went up a hill? I don't understand that."

"Aloysius didn't say up a hill," Susannah said, "he said into a hill. The Lady's Hill. It's different."

"So?" Danny said. "You don't know where it is, anyway. You don't know where this *vieja* is. We could walk for days and never find her! What are we gonna eat? And drink? I didn't have any breakfast."

"All I had was one and a half bananas."

Danielle flapped a hand. "How we gonna know where this old lady lives?"

"I know she lives in the woods," Susannah said. "Danny, we'll find her. People find each other in stories. I found *you*. I didn't know you were here, I found you."

"That's true," conceded Danielle. She put her hand to her throat. "Hey. I got my lucky stone. I grabbed it before I left the house."

Danielle's lucky stone looked like a plain old gray stone, but it was special. It had a hole all the way through it. Danny had found it on the beach one Sunday afternoon and stuck it in her pocket. Celie had given her a strand of leather cord to thread it on so that she could wear it around her neck when she needed luck.

"That's great," Susannah said. "Maybe it will be magic here."

"You think so?" Danny's eyes brightened. "You know, Mom says there's no such thing as magic—" She giggled.

Susannah grinned.

A black bird with red wings flew past them. It perched on the branch ahead of them, watching them from one eye. "That's the first bird I've seen," Susannah said.

"We better be careful," said Danny. "There might be wild animals in this forest."

"I guess," Susannah said, but she wasn't worried. All the animals she had met so far had been odd, but friendly. She wondered where Mr. D was. Still in the jungle, perhaps, having cat adventures.

Blue sky shone through the treetops, making patches of sunlight on the pine needles. A second bird flew by them and lighted on a branch. It swung there, singing. It was blue.

"Look." Danny pointed. In a nearby tree, two bushy-tailed, beady-eyed squirrels were discussing a nut. The blue bird sang a trill. "This is better," Danny said.

Susannah agreed. The forest was brighter now. The trees were less tall. The trunks of the trees had interesting patterns on them. Even the needles on the ground were different; they were a wonderful color, not red or orange or brown or coral, but a color Susannah had never seen. . . .

Plop!

A pine cone fell at Susannah's feet.

Picking it up, she threw it. It was light as a leaf. It arced through the trees and vanished. The bird trilled again.

"This way!" Susannah loped after the cone. She found it on the ground ahead of her, right in the middle of the path. She threw it again, followed—and stopped.

Danny caught up with her and stood beside her, panting.

In a clearing in the forest stood a small gray house.

Chapter Five

                   "Hey," Danielle said, "that looks like my house!"

The house did look a little like Danielle's house. It was two-storied, with a peaked roof, a porch and two bay windows. It had funny wooden carvings over it, just like the houses on Allan Street.

Like Danny's house it was painted gray. The chimney stones were gray. A gray plume of smoke drifted up through the sunlight and was lost in the treetops' shadows.

A gray gate stood in front of the house. It stood as if it were attached to a fence, but there was no fence—just the gate. A bunch of chickens pecked and scratched beside a woodpile at the side of the house. The chickens were all different colors: red and brown and white.

"I think we're here," Danny said.

Susannah nodded.

"Someone's cooking," Danny said. She sniffed. "I can smell it. There must be someone home." Cupping both hands around her mouth, she shouted, "Hello!"

The front door opened. A woman emerged and walked toward them. She wore gray, too: a gray skirt to her ankles, a gray top, and she had gray eyes. Her hair was long and sparrow-brown.

She's not old, Susannah realized. She's not as old as Mother. She's just an older girl.

The girl walked to the other side of the gate. "You're Susannah," she said. "You're Danny. I'm Sarah. I've been waiting for you."

Susannah thought: This is a witch's house.

Witches came into most of the stories she had ever heard, and most of them were mean or bad.

Still, if you were having an Adventure, you had to be *in* it.

"Does the Old Woman live here?" she asked.

The gray-eyed girl smiled. "Yes. Her name is Mother Bea." She stepped back. "Would you like to come in?"

"How do we come in?"

"Through the gate. Just push to open it."

Susannah looked at Danny. Danny shrugged. Susannah bit her lower lip. Finally she laid her hand on the gate and pushed. It swung inward. With Danny right behind her, she stepped through. "Come," Sarah said. They followed her across the clearing and up the porch steps. Behind them, the gate swung shut, all by itself.

The front door was gray. At first glance it looked like the front door of any house. The only odd thing about it was the door knocker, which was long and black and shaped like—like a *nose.*

"That's weird," said Danny. "Imagine knocking on a door with someone's nose."

"I wouldn't," Susannah said. The knocker had no mouth or eyes or chin. It was just a nose jutting from the wooden door.

"You'd better not!" said a deep voice. It was not Sarah's. The girls looked around, and then up, but saw no one. Susannah looked at Sarah. She smiled.

"Open," she said.

"Don't wanna," said the voice. "You have no idea how boring it is to do just one thing, swing open, swing shut, all day . . ." But as the voice spoke the gray door opened by itself. Two eyes and a mouth formed themselves around the nose. The eyes stared at Susannah.

"Who're you?" said the mouth.

"Susannah," said Susannah.

The eyes—they were brown—rolled to look at Danielle. "Who's she?"

"I'm Danny," Danielle said. "Who're you?"

"I'm the door, stupid," said the mouth with grumpy satisfaction. Things in Storyland are sure rude! Susannah thought, remembering the gibbon.

"I didn't know doors could talk," Danny said.

"I bet there's a lot you don't know," said the door. "Are you coming in or not?"

"Yes!" Danny marched in front of Susannah and walked into the house. Susannah followed. Sarah came behind Susannah.

"Shut," she said. The door shut.

Susannah looked around the house. She wondered nervously if everything in it was alive and could talk to her. At first glance the house looked very ordinary: it had a hallway going back and doorways leading off the hallway, just like Susannah's own house.

"Come," Sarah said, gesturing to the first doorway on the left. "We'll wait for Mother Bea. She's out. But she knew you'd be coming. She'll be back."

Susannah swallowed. "Is Mother Bea a witch?"

Sarah smiled. "Of course."

"Are you?"

Sarah shook her head. "Not yet. I'm her apprentice. I'm learning."

The room on the left was warm and sunny. Plants in pots dangled from chains in the middle of the bay window. Under the plants there was a big wooden table. There were three big armchairs—one red, one blue, and one brown—a bookshelf with lots of books, a cabinet with a great carved door, and a fireplace. Next to the fireplace stood a small wooden stool. Sarah went to it and sat, folding her skirt around her ankles.

A round iron pot hung in the fireplace. Cauldron, Susannah thought. A witch's pot was called a cauldron. She wondered what was in the cauldron. It smelled good. Tentatively she sat on the arm of the red armchair.

Danny pointed to a huge book. It lay open on a stand. "What's this?"

"That's a grimoire," said Sarah. "A magic book."

Danielle stepped back from the stand. "Oh. What's that?" She pointed to a dirty metal pitcher sitting on the table. It looked like an old cream pot.

"That's the djinn's lamp. If you rub it, he'll come out."

Danielle put her hands behind her back hastily. "Oh. What's that?" She pointed with her chin to a long dangly thing over the doorway.

"That's a sliver of the skin of Ouroboros, the Great Worm. He sheds it every two thousand years."

"Ugh," said Danielle. She sat on the other arm of the red chair. "Is everything here magic?"

"Mostly," Sarah said.

51

"What do you do? Do you do magic?"

"I keep the fire going and I watch the mirror." Sarah nodded toward an oval mirror. It hung in a silver frame on the wall.

Susannah squinted at it, but all it showed her was the room, Sarah, Danny, and herself. "Is it magic?" she asked.

"Yes," Sarah said. "Sometimes things that happen, or are going to happen, or have happened, or *might* happen, are reflected in the mirror. I remember them. When Mother Bea asks I tell her what I see."

"What's that," Danny asked, pointing across the room to what looked like a ladder. It disappeared into a hole in the ceiling.

"That's the ladder to the loft. That's where I sleep."

"Ooh." Danielle jumped up. "Can I look?"

"Go ahead. Climb it if you like."

Danielle walked to the ladder and laid a hand on a rung. "Come with me," she said to Susannah.

"Okay." Susannah rose. Danielle scrambled up the ladder to the hole. Susannah followed slowly.

As Susannah poked her head through the hole, something green and sweet-smelling struck her gently on the cheek. She put a hand up, gazing into the loft. Long strings of dry plants hung from the beams. She pulled herself up three more steps. "Where are you?" she called.

"Here," Danny said. "At the window."

Susannah climbed two more steps to the loft floor. Stepping from the ladder, she gazed at the loft. It was shaped like a capital A. On the sides the ceiling slanted, but in the middle it was high enough for a tall person to stand erect. Against one wall lay a bed with a quilt and a pillow. Near it sat a wooden chest, like Niall's toy chest, except that it was brown, not purple.

A round window had been cut into the slanted wall over the bed. It had no glass. Above it was a rolled up curtain. Danielle knelt on the bed, looking out.

"Come see," she said, holding out a hand. "This is boss."

Susannah crossed the loft and knelt at Danielle's side. "You only like it because it's high."

"I think it would be neat to live here," Danny said. "Can you see? Look!"

Susannah looked out the window.

Everything was very small, as if she was standing on the top of a very high place. She saw the yard, the gate, the chickens. . . . She could even see beyond the trees. It was like a movie: there was the grassy plain to which she had fallen, and the tree under which she slept. That bright blotch was the jungle. Beyond the jungle was a river, and beyond the river a glittery smudge which as she stared resolved itself into houses and park and skyscrapers and a red and yellow streetcar rattling up a hill—

She was looking, somehow, at San Francisco.

She pulled her head in quickly, feeling dizzy. "It's magic."

"Yeah," Danielle said. Her voice was soft with wonder. "Did you see it? Chomolungma?"

"Is that what you saw?"

Danny nodded. Her eyes were bright.

"I saw San Francisco."

Suddenly a voice spoke below them. "Children," it said, "come down."

Susannah's stomach lurched. "It's the witch."

Danny stuck her chin out. "So?" She swung bravely down the ladder. Susannah followed her. She felt strange. What if the witch wouldn't help them look for Niall? What if she was mean, or cruel, or evil?

The ladder ended too soon. Susannah took a deep breath and turned around to face the witch.

Wow, she thought. She's *tall*.

The witch stood in front of her cauldron. She wore a black, shapeless piece of clothing that went from her neck to her feet. Her toes poked beneath the hem. They were yellow and bare. She was very thin, with gray hair and stern dark eyes and skin that seemed papery, like the pages of an old book.

She leaned on a black wooden cane. Its handle was carved in the shape of a bird.

"I am Mother Bea," she said.

Her voice was deep and calm. Susannah's stomach relaxed. Feeling very small, she made a curtsy. Danny put one hand over her heart and the other behind her back and made a choppy bow.

"I'm Susannah," Susannah said, and then felt foolish. A witch would know their names. Sarah had known their names. But it was better to be polite than to stand and say nothing like a dummy. "This is my friend Danielle. Danny."

"Pleasetomeetcha."

Mother Bea smiled.

"I know who you are," she said. "You have never met a witch before and are wondering what to do. Don't worry. I'll tell you." She pointed a bony finger toward the table. "First you must say hello to an old friend."

Susannah turned.

Folded up on the table, looking smug, was Mr. D.

"Mr. D!" Susannah went toward him, hand outstretched. He blinked at her and, rising, came to butt his head against her chest. She rubbed her thumb along the line of his pink nose.

"We met in the woods," said the witch. "He told me he was looking for some friends of his, and I invited him here."

"Was he looking for me?" Susannah said.

"He mentioned your name."

Danny said, "You mean, he *talked*?"

Mother Bea said, "You have met a door that talks. Why does it surprise you that a cat might talk?"

"He didn't before," Danny said.

"Not to you. Cats are particular about who they talk to."

"Mowr," said Mr. D. He waved his tail. Susannah wondered if he

55

was saying, "That's right!" in Cat. He opened his mouth, snapped it shut, and butted Susannah's hand.

"He wants to eat," she said.

"See," said the witch. "You know what he said. How about you? Would you like lunch?"

Susannah wondered, Was it safe to eat the food in a witch's house? There was a story about a magic island where people ate and were turned into pigs . . .

"I do," Danny said.

"Me too," said a sulky voice.

"You always want lunch," said Mother Bea. She held up her walking stick. The carved bird on the handle turned its head from one side to the other.

"Do you like chicken?" said Mother Bea.

"Yum," said Danny.

"I like chicken," said the wooden bird.

"Be quiet," said the witch. The bird blinked, and stiffened into immobility. "Sarah, get cutlery." Sarah rose from her stool. Opening the cupboard, she removed spoons and forks and knives and laid them round the table. Mr. D, watching, lifted his head and meowed imperiously. Sarah took a bowl from the cupboard and put it at the big cat's side.

"Chairs," said Mother Bea.

The blue armchair began to shake. Then it split itself neatly into two tall-backed kitchen chairs. The chairs waddled to the table.

"Sit down."

Danny and Susannah sat.

"Milk," said the witch. A blue pitcher popped out of the air onto the table. "And mugs." Two blue mugs appeared. A marvelous smell filled the room. It smelled like beans. The pitcher rose into the air over the mugs, and then tipped. Milk poured into the first one, then the other mug. "Do you like rice?"

"Yes," the children said together. Two plates sailed from the cupboard to hover over the pot. Picking up a ladle, Mother Bea ladled burritos, rice, and beans from the cauldron to the plates. When she was done, the plates floated through the air and landed on the table.

Danny stared from her plate to the pot. "How does it do that?" she demanded. "You can't have rice and beans and chicken and tortillas mixed up in there. You'd just get mush!"

Mother Bea laid a slice of white chicken meat in Mr. D's bowl. "My pot holds anything I want it to."

Susannah said, "I never heard of a witch who fed people burritos."

The food was delicious. Danny took seconds. After both children finished, the dishes floated into the air and vanished into the iron pot. When they came out again, they were sparkling clean. "A dishwasher!" said Danny. "Wow. My mom would love to have that pot."

"I think you have to be a witch," Susannah said.

"That's right," said Mother Bea. "Stack yourselves," she told the plates. They floated serenely into their shelf in the cupboard. "Children, stand up." Susannah and Danielle stood. The two kitchen chairs turned back into the blue armchair.

Mr. D, looking sated, perched on the table, washing his face with a paw.

"Thank you," Susannah said. "That was good."

"For sure," Danny said.

"You're welcome," said the witch. "Food is important. Adventurers need steady hearts and full bellies." She looked keenly at Susannah.

Susannah swallowed. Her heart thumped in her chest. She did not feel especially brave or steady, though she was certainly full. This, she knew, was the place in the story where the witch or wizard told the adventurers what the rest of the adventure would be.

Danny said, "Are you gonna help us find Susannah's brother? That's what we came here for, you know."

"I know," said the witch. She lifted the cane. "Look." She pointed the head of the cane toward the mirror in the silver frame. She said something soft. The mirror's surface shimmered. When it cleared, there was Niall in bed, in the house in San Francisco. As they watched, he woke, ran down the hall, opened the door, and scampered down the steps to the sidewalk of Allan Street.

"Stupid brat," Susannah muttered.

Danny said, "It's like TV!" She watched Niall run along the sidewalk toward the park. "What's he doing?"

"He's following the Silver Horse," said the witch. And there in the mirror was the horse. Its coat was glowing silver. Its eyes were ruby red. It neighed, and cantered through the park. "The horse isn't really a toy, of course. He is the steed of the Dreamkeeper. She rides him on the nights she comes to visit your world, when the moon is full. But he loves to play alone in the moonlight, like any magic thing. Last month he galloped alone at moonset around the edge of the sky and was trapped by dawn and turned into wood. Last night, when the moon was full again, the Dreamkeeper called him home."

"Where is his home?" Susannah whispered.

"In the Dreamkeeper's Hill."

"Who is that—the Dreamkeeper?" Danny said. "What does she do?"

Mother Bea pointed at the mirror. It shimmered.

A woman stood within the frame. She had white, white skin. Her hair was so pale that it seemed to be made of snow. Her eyes were light gray. She wore a glittering lacy gown that wrapped around her like a cloud. The only color about her was a green stone that gleamed in a silver ring on her right hand. She was looking out through the mirror, smiling as if she could see them through its enchanted surface.

"She's beautiful," Danny said. Her shoulders hunched. "She looks mean, though."

"Is she a witch too?" asked Susannah.

"She is. She is empress of the dreamfolk who people the dreams of mortals. They live in her kingdom beneath the Hill. At night she sends them forth. When the moon is full she sometimes rides herself into the real world to trouble the dreams of human men and women." The mirror's surface shimmered. "Now look."

"That's Niall!" Susannah cried. Framed in silver, he sat on a white rug in a white, white room. "Where is he? What's he doing?"

"Niall is not doing," said the witch. "He is dreaming. The Silver Horse brought him beneath the Hill."

Susannah stared at her brother. Niall's eyes were vacant. His hands rested quietly on his lap. He looks like a zombie, she thought. "What's the matter with him? Why doesn't he move?"

"He doesn't want to move. He wants to dream. As he dreams," the witch said, "he forgets. Soon he will not remember that he ever lived anywhere else."

"That's weird," Danny said.

"It's an unkind thing the Dreamkeeper has done. But Niall is not the first mortal to be lured beneath the Hill and trapped in dreaming."

Susannah stared into the mirror. Niall's dreambound face frightened her. "Will she let him go?"

Mother Bea shook her head gravely. "If you wish your brother back, Susannah, you must go to him. You must wake him from the dream and bring him with you out of the Hill."

Jeanne Gomoll

Chapter Six

Out of the Hill . . . Out of the
Hill . . . The words echoed. On the wall, the mirror shimmered
and changed. Susannah saw her own face in it. It looked very
small. Over her shoulder Mother Bea was looking at her in the

mirror. The witch's bony yellow hands were folded over the handle of her cane.

I can't do it, Susannah thought. I'm not a witch; I can't do magic. I'm a kid. It's not my fault he's there. I don't want to do it. What if I get trapped in the Hill? My mother and father will worry if I don't come home.

But she knew they would be equally worried about Niall. He was so little. . . .

"Do you want him back?" said Mother Bea.

No, Susannah thought rebelliously, he's a brat. But she knew that wasn't fair. He was only six. And even if he was a brat, he was her brother. She couldn't leave him in a strange place with that empty look on his face. Lifting her head, she faced the witch. "Yes," she answered. "I do."

The witch's severe face grew gentler. "Good. You must want him, or your endeavor will fail."

"I want him," Susannah said. "Stupid brat." She squared her shoulders. "You'll have to tell me how to get in there, but I'll get him."

"Hey!" Danielle punched Susannah's arm. "You're not going anywhere alone. *I'm* here." She stuck her chin out at the witch. "I'm going too."

Mother Bea smiled. "I know you are, Danielle."

Susannah grinned at her friend with love. "I'm glad you're with me."

"Will *you* come?" Danny asked the witch.

Mother Bea shook her head. "No. I have no power in Dreamland."

"But you're a witch!"

"I am. But so is the Lady of the Hill, and she does not want me there. Were I to even set foot past the entrance to Dreamland, the very walls would call out, crying warning and challenge. You, being mortals, can enter freely and they will not speak. She will not know of your presence in the dreamworld until she returns."

"You mean she isn't there?" Susannah said.

"That's right. She rides the Horse tonight, troubling some poor mortal's dream. She will not return until the dawn."

"But aren't there magic creatures in the Hill?" Susannah said. "Goblins and gremlins and—"

"As long as you are steadfast, what you meet in Dreamland cannot hurt you."

"What does that mean?" said Danielle.

Mother Bea's dark eyes seemed to glow. "It means that you must not be trapped in Dreamland. Dreams are beautiful and potent. The dreamfolk will try to entrance you to stay, to give up your own desires and to be satisfied with dreams. You must remain strong. You must want to leave them!"

"We won't want to stay," Danny said. "Who wants to dream all the time?"

"Some people do," the witch said gravely.

"Which is the real world?" Susannah said. "Storyland? Dreamland? Or the world we came from—the park, Allan Street, San Francisco?"

"A good question," said the witch. "All are real. But when folk from the dreamworld live in your world, they become ghosts. When mortals live in the dreamworld, they become myths. Storyland is the only place where mortals, dreamfolk, and their beasts and toys may meet and return to their own worlds."

"Is Dreamland a part of Storyland?" Susannah asked.

"All places are a part of Storyland."

"But if all places are a part of Storyland, then is our world a story? Whose story?"

The witch smiled.

Danny said practically, "So there are people in the dreamworld. Will they help us find Niall?"

"They may. You may help them."

"What about the dreams? Will they help us?"

"Help you! Hurt you! Awk!" said the wooden bird.

"They may do either," said the witch. "They may not notice you are there."

"Will we see them? You said they were ghosts."

"They are only ghosts in your world. They are the empress's subjects, the inhabitants of her kingdom. They are numerous."

Susannah frowned. "How will we know who to trust?" she asked.

"Awk! Use your brains!"

"Quiet," said Mother Bea. The command shivered through the house. The bird bowed its head and was still.

"Maybe," Susannah said, "maybe you could send someone with us. To help."

"No one can do more than you can."

"We can't do magic."

"You don't need magic. You would not know how to use it."

A woman spoke. "Give them iron."

Susannah and Danielle both jumped, and looked around to see who—or what—was speaking. Mother Bea and Sarah looked up. Susannah looked up too. All she saw was the ceiling. It was dusty. One corner even held a spiderweb.

"Do you think so, Anansi?" said Mother Bea, in a tone of deep respect.

"Who's she talking to?" Danielle whispered.

"Iron," said the invisible presence, "breaks illusion. Iron or stone."

Mother Bea nodded. "Good advice, as always. Thank you, Anansi."

Danielle said, "Who are you talking to?"

Mother Bea's papery face creased in a brief smile. "To Anansi, my friend and colleague."

"Where is she? I don't see anyone."

"She is there." The witch pointed to the spiderweb.

Susannah licked her lips. Her mouth felt dry. "The spider? The spider talks?"

A laugh floated from the corner. "As well as you, child." The spiderweb quivered. A large black spider sat in the middle of it. "You have met a door that talks, why not a spider?"

Susannah said, "Are you—are you a witch, too?"

"No," said the spider. Her voice was rich with amusement. "I am a familiar. And you waste time conversing with me. You have an errand to do in the Hill!"

Mother Bea said, "Iron or stone will hold the dreamfolk off should they try to stop you in your search. But you must have brought it with you. What do you have in your pockets, Susannah?"

"Nothing," Susannah said. She had emptied the pockets of her jeans before going to bed. "But Danny has stuff!"

"Show me."

Danielle pulled everything out of her pockets and laid it on the table: string, sand dollar, snail shell, a brown pebble, some pine needles, the pen cap, the pocket knife. . . . "It isn't much," she said.

"It will do." Mother Bea pushed the shell, sand dollar, and pen cap to one side. She picked up the pebble, examined it, laid it down. Then she pointed, first at the knife and then at the bits of string, and spoke. Her words were like no language that Susannah had ever heard before.

The room went dark. Susannah gasped, and grabbed Danny's hand.

The light came back.

On the table, instead of a pocket knife and four pieces of string, was a leather belt with a leather loop hanging from it. Inside the loop was a shiny blue-bladed axe. The blade was oddly shaped; it reminded Susannah of a bird's head. "Oh," Susannah said. She was disappointed. She had expected to see a sword or a light saber, like in *Star Wars*.

Danny snatched it up. "Bitchin!" she said. "An ice axe. I want this."

"You may have it," Mother Bea said. "The dreamfolk dislike

iron and will not approach it. It can be a weapon, but try not to use it. You go to the Hill to rescue, not to hurt."

Danny picked up the belt and slid it into her jeans. "I understand," she said. "What about Susannah?"

"I don't want an axe," Susannah said.

"You have to have something," Danny argued. "It isn't fair."

The bird on the handle of the witch's cane flapped its wings. "Send me! I have sharp eyes. I'll find the human boy."

"You would be no help at all," Mother Bea said. "The empress would see you and freeze you to the canopy of her throne."

Abashed, the bird stuck its head beneath one wing.

From overhead, Anansi said, "Danielle wears stone against her throat."

Mother Bea looked at Danny. "My lucky stone," Danny said, putting a hand to her neck. "I found it on the beach."

"Let me see it."

Danny gathered the thong in both hands and lifted it over her head.

Mother Bea held the stone to the light. She turned it in her fingers. She smelled it. At last she touched it with the tip of her tongue. "Anansi, what think you?" she said.

"It will do," said the spider. "It's a thing of earth; it's strong."

Mother Bea turned to Danny. "Danielle, will you permit Susannah to take your lucky stone and wear it through Dreamland?"

Danny scowled.

Quickly Susannah said, "I don't need anything. Danny should keep the stone. It's hers."

Anansi said, "Danny has the axe."

Danielle's scowl grew stronger; it made her eyebrows point down and her lips twist. Her lower lip bulged out. "No!" she said. "It isn't fair for me to have two things. You take it." But she did not look at Susannah as she said it.

"You are sure," said the witch.

"I'm sure."

"Good." Mother Bea dangled the stone over the cauldron. Dipping the stone into the pot, she spoke in that strange harsh language. Then she lifted her hand. "Take it," she said, extending the stone to Susannah.

Susannah took it. It was dry as bone, and seemed unchanged. "What'll it do?" she asked, putting it over her head.

"It will help you gauge whom to trust," said the witch. "If you doubt the motives or truthfulness of any you meet in the Hill, watch the stone. In the presence of falsehood it will change color."

Susannah closed her hand around the stone. "Thank you."

"Are you ready to go?"

"Now?"

"Right now," Mother Bea said.

"I'm ready," said Danielle.

Mr. D was observing her from his perch on the table top. "You want to come with us, cat?" Susannah said softly. It had worked before in the grasslands. But the cat turned his head and pretended to be looking out the window. Susannah made her spine stiff. It was too late to be scared.

"Ready," she said.

"Sarah will guide you to the door into the Hill. There is only one way into the Hill and one way out for mortal folk, and they are the same. The dreamfolk serve their empress; be careful to whom you reveal your errand! And remember, only your own desires can trap you. You must want to come back!"

"That is the Hill," Sarah said.

They stood at the edge of the forest. Behind them lay shadow. In front of them a bright green strip of lawn lay bathed in sunlight. It was brighter than the grass on a golf course. Susannah had never seen a color so bright. On the other side of the lawn stood a bare hummock, a smooth arching mound of earth. It was covered with a soft gray mist. As the girls followed Sarah onto the grass, the mist seemed to retreat from them.

Sarah pointed to a blot of darkness on the mound. "That's the door."

Susannah squinted. It looked like the entrance to a cave. "How big is the Hill?" The Hill might be much bigger than it looked. They could get lost.

"It's big," Sarah said. "But time works differently under the Hill. If you keep to your errand, you can find your brother and be back in your world before the moon has set." She raised a hand. "I wish you luck."

"I wish you could come with us," Susannah said.

Sarah shook her head. "I will watch you in the mirror."

"Hey." Danny joggled Susannah's arm.

Stalking purposefully across the grass to them was the big orange cat.

"You coming with us, Mr. D?" said Susannah when he reached them. He rubbed his head on her knee and purred. "Good."

"Why? What can he do? He's only a cat," said Danny.

"There's no such thing as 'only a cat.'" Susannah bent to rub Mr. D's nose. "Cats are magic." I hope they are, she thought.

"Good-bye," said Sarah. She walked toward the pines. The instant she stepped off the lawn, the mist began to advance from the Hill. Soon Susannah could barely see the lawn or the mound or the trees behind her. Only the brown top of the mound showed through the soupy mist.

Danielle stared at it. "I don't like this stuff," she grumbled.

"It's just fog, like at home." But they both knew this fog was nothing like San Francisco fog.

"Well," Danny said, "let's do it." Rubbing her arms, she marched toward the dark shadow on the mound. Bravely she poked a fist into the darkness.

"Ugh," she said. "It's just empty."

There was no going back.

67

"I'll go first," Danny said.

"No. I will," said Susannah. "He's my brother." They glared at each other. At that moment Mr. D, tail held high, slipped between them and padded into the dark.

"Come on!" said Susannah. She held out a hand.

Danny grabbed it.

The entrance was so low that they had to duck their heads. A grown-up would have had to bend double. One hand in front of her to feel for edges and bumps, Susannah moved cautiously into the tunnel. It was so dark that she kept squeezing her eyes shut just to see the pinwheeling colors form on her eyelids.

Something warm and soft brushed her reaching hand. "Hello, magic cat," she said.

The tunnel made her voice sound spooky. "Where's the cat?" Danny asked.

"Right in front of me."

"Cats are good in the dark," Danny said hopefully.

Susannah doubted that even a cat could see in this thick darkness, but she wasn't sure. She shuffled forward a few steps. The tunnel roof lifted; she could stand. The flat smooth floor was easy to walk on even in the dark. The air smelled old.

Danny was gripping her hand very hard. "You okay?" Susannah asked.

"Yeah," Danny said. She sounded as if she was trying not to cough.

"Let go of my hand and hold on to my waist. Then I can feel ahead with both hands."

"Okay," Danny said. "Stand still." Susannah stood. Danny released her hand and grabbed one of her belt loops. "How's that?"

"Better." Susannah worked her cramped hand until the blood tingled through it. She reached out. The tunnel wall was gritty on her palms. "I wonder how long this lasts."

"Me too."

Danny's voice still sounded tight. She's scared, Susannah

thought. How come I'm not scared? I guess it's because I've read more stories.

"It can't last too long," she said. "I'm sure Mother Bea would have told us. It's not so bad. I always thought caves were cold, but this is warm."

"Yeah," said Danny. "It's not so bad. Want to switch?"

"Okay." They changed places. Danny got in front. Susannah tucked her fingers into the stiff leather of the enchanted belt. It was hard to move without bumping into Danny or stepping on her heels. It didn't seem to matter whether her eyes were open or closed. She closed them experimentally. Then she opened them. Stupid, you didn't close your eyes in an Adventure! If you did, something came from behind a rock and ate you.

"Hey," Danny said, stopping suddenly. "I see lights."

Jeanne Gomoll

Chapter Seven

Susannah peered around Danny's shoulder. "See?" Danny said. "They look like Christmas lights."
Susannah rubbed her eyes with the heels of her hands. "I don't see anything," she muttered. She stared. She did see something:

points of light which gleamed orange and red and blue. She wondered if they were real. "Keep going. Maybe they'll disappear."

"You think so?" Danny shuffled forward.

The sparkles did not vanish. They grew brighter. "I can see my hands," Danny whispered. "Wow, look at that!" They had reached the sparkles. Blue, red, and amber jewels glittered in the rock walls of the tunnel. The walls were not dark but swirling with colors. The colors' names—sandy ocher and carmine red and indigo—rolled into Susannah's mind as if she were reading them off her paint box. Pillars of rock, big as the trunks of trees, jutted from the smooth rock floor.

Spikes hung from the ceiling. Stalactites, Susannah thought, or were they stalagmites? She could never remember. She brushed her fingers across the multicolored rock. It was warm.

"Now where's that cat?" Danny said.

Susannah turned in a circle. Mr. D had vanished. Probably gone exploring. "Don't worry about him," she said, remembering how he had wandered away from her in the jungle and then turned up in the witch's house. "He'll find us when he wants us."

"Look at that!" Danielle pointed to one twisting strand of sapphires imbedded in the rock wall above their heads. "It would make a bitchin necklace."

"It's like looking at constellations. Remember the field trip to the planetarium?"

"I wonder who built it." Danielle stroked the rock. A dreamy look entered her eyes. "You know, I bet I could climb this. I could go up here—and here—and pry out one of those blue stones and take it home for my mom." She slid her hand toward the ice axe. "I can use this. It's for ice, but that's okay. It won't take long. You wait here." She slipped the axe from its loop.

Susannah grabbed her wrist. "Danny, don't! You might fall and hurt yourself!"

"I won't fall!" Danny's eyes blazed. "I never fall. I climb all the time at Land's End and on the rocks at Corona Heights and I've never fallen."

"But this place is magic," Susannah said. "The walls might have a spell on them."

"Huh. My axe is magic. It can protect me." Danielle ran her hand over the rock as if she were looking for a place to start.

No, Susannah thought desperately, this is wrong. I know it. "Danny, don't," she said. "We're in a hurry, remember? We have to find Niall and leave before the Dreamkeeper comes back. And that axe isn't for climbing, it's for chasing away dream people if they try to stop us."

Danny's scowl twisted her eyebrows. She stared at the tunnel wall a moment. Then she muttered, "Yeah. Yeah, okay." Turning, she glared over her shoulder. "Well, come on. You want to find Niall? Don't just stand there!"

Fooey, Susannah wanted to say, don't boss me around! This is *my* Adventure. But she followed. They went deeper into the painted tunnel. The jewels burned like flames in their niches. The upthrusting rocks looked like bizarre animal heads.

Danielle put her hands on her hips. "Hello!" she called. There was no response. She turned in a circle. "You know, this place is beautiful but it's really boring." She craned her neck to stare at the toothy rocks.

One spike hung almost low enough to touch. A blue jewel glowed at its tip. "I'm gonna get that," Danny said. Sliding her axe from its loop, she crouched and jumped, batting at the jewel with the axe head. The jewel sprang from the rock and bounced off the multicolored floor.

Kneeling, Danny scooped it into her palm. "Yeow!" She shook it from her hand. It rolled a little ways and stopped, still shining. "It burns." She licked her fingertips and blew on them.

"You okay?"

"Yeah." Danny stared at her feet. "Now where did it go?" But the jewel had disappeared into a crack. She rose. "That thing was hot."

"Like the walls."

They continued walking. Suddenly Danny, in front, jumped back. "Ugh!"

"What is it?"

"It looks like—like bones."

"What! Let me see." Susannah stepped forward.

Directly across their path, a human skeleton lay on the colorful stone floor.

The skin on Susannah's neck and arms prickled with chill. Piles of dark pebbles lay all around the bones. The skeleton's left arm rested tidily beside the ribs on one side. The right reached above the domed white skull, almost touching the wall. The jaw grinned. The wide mouth had no teeth. The bones lay neatly, as if the person had died while asleep. The colors of the floor shone through the arched rib bones.

"You think it's real?" Danny whispered.

"I don't know," Susannah said. She knelt.

"Susannah, don't touch it, it's gross!"

"I won't," Susannah said. "I just want to look." She leaned forward. "I don't think it's gross."

This close she could see the bones were yellow, not white like Halloween skeletons were. She bent closer. The lucky stone banged her on the chest. She closed a hand around it. Then, on impulse, she drew it over her head and held it near the bones.

Nothing happened.

Maybe it isn't working, she thought. It's supposed to change color if the bones aren't real.

Maybe it is working.

Danielle said, "How come there are pebbles all over the place?"

"I don't know." Susannah picked one up.

Faintly, like a flashlight bulb that was almost dead, it began to glow blue. "Look!" Susannah held it out to Danny. "It's like the jewels."

Danny stared at it. She prodded it with a finger. "Is it hot?"

"It's warm."

"Close your hand." Susannah closed her fist around the jewel. It grew warm. Warmer. Hot! Opening her fingers, Susannah let it roll from her palm. It fell to the floor. The blue glow faded, faded. . . . In a moment she could not tell it from the other pebbles on the floor.

Danielle said, "There are no jewels in the wall around the bones." Susannah glanced upward. It was true. "He must have taken them out of the wall to take home." She frowned. "But why did he stay here? Why didn't he leave?"

"I don't know," Susannah said. "Maybe he tried to climb, and fell."

Danielle stuck her chin out. "Huh." She stared at the bones and then, stretching, took a big step over them. "Come on." She held out a hand. "Let's go."

They kept walking. The tunnel was still beautiful but the presence of the bones made Susannah wonder what might be hidden in it. The jewel patterns seemed to shift confusingly. The warm air was stagnant and musty.

Suddenly Susannah felt a delicious cool breeze on her cheeks. Sniffing, she followed it to an archway in the rock. "Danny!"

"Yo!"

"Let's go this way." Susannah pointed at the archway.

"Okay," Danny said. Shoulders touching, they walked through the arch into a huge, white cavern.

The walls were white. The ceiling, which dripped with spikes like giant icicles, was white. The floor was white and hard and covered with tall pillars. Danielle pointed wordlessly to a pillar shaped like a tree. It had a trunk and branches and pale white leaves. But the leaves did not move in the breeze, nor did the branches. Everything was quiet and very still.

"Niall was in a white place."

"Yes. And that *bruja*, that witch, wore white. I think we're here."

They walked between two of the frozen trees. Suddenly, soundlessly, a woman glided across their path. Susannah squeaked.

"Ssh!" said Danielle. The woman turned her head and smiled. She wore a long white skirt, a ruffled white blouse, and a white hat with a feather on it. Her face, hair and eyes were pale as quartz.

"That's not the witch," Danny said.

"She must be a dream person," Susannah said. "I wonder why this place has no colors." She looked at Danny's brown skin and black hair. "We sure stand out. Everyone can see us. It's going to be hard to find Niall without everyone here knowing it."

"That lady didn't seem to care about us," Danny said. "She just went wherever she was going. Maybe they can't see us. Maybe we're invisible."

"She smiled at us."

"Oh, yeah."

A second dream person drifted in front of them. He wore a long robe with big square sleeves, and a tall hat. He carried a cane. He sketched a bow at the two girls and drifted on. His eyes were empty, like glass.

Slowly the dreamfolk emerged. People of all kinds, in different costumes, strolled about the cavern. Animals roamed among them, equally silent: cats and horses and dogs. A big pale snake slithered past them. Danielle jumped, and clutched Susannah's arm. A great winged horse trotted through the cave. A man as tall as a house stalked near them. He did not look at them or even appear to know that they were there.

"Paul Bunyan," Susannah said.

"Abiyoyo," Danny suggested. Shapes of fantasy—lions, dwarfs, giant birds, a dog with three heads—filled the icebound cave. "This place is *freaky*."

75

Bright as a small sun, an orange cat marched from between two pillars and began to wash his face.

"Mr. D!" Susannah ran forward to greet the cat. "Oh, Mr. D." Kneeling, she stroked him. He licked her hand and went back to smoothing his whiskers. "Mr. D, have you seen Niall?"

"Greetings," said a soft voice behind them. "Are you looking for someone? Perhaps I may help."

The children turned.

A man stood watching them. He looked like someone out of a story. He wore an icy dazzle of silk. His face was white. His powdered hair was tied with silver ribbons. There were silver rings on his pale hands. He was even wearing, at his left side, a sword. His eyes were no color. They reminded Susannah of the Dreamkeeper's eyes.

Mr. D stopped washing his face. He curled his tail around his paws, diamond eyes alert.

"Welcome to the Hill of Dreams," the man said. "Seldom are we host to visitors from the mortal world."

He had a wonderful voice. It sounded as if he were singing, not speaking. It reminded Susannah of Mother Bea's voice. He seemed more solid than the other pale folk who floated wraith-like through the cave.

If he was not a dream person, he might be human. "Hi," Susannah said. "Uh, greetings."

He smiled at her. "You are new come to the Hill, I think. I have not seen you before."

"We just got here."

Danny's elbow whacked Susannah's side, hard. She was staring at the man, her chin jutting out. "Hey!" Susannah said.

"Don't talk to him." Danielle sounded angry.

"Why not?"

"I don't like him. I don't trust him. He feels wrong."

"I was trying to be polite," Susannah said. Did he feel wrong? She wasn't sure. No one else had talked to them. She let her hand

creep up to the stone. She wondered how to use it. She couldn't just walk up to someone and say, *"Excuse me, but I need to know if you're human."*

The man watched them, smiling. "May I know your names, mortals?"

Susannah started to answer, but Danny interrupted her. "Who are you?"

"I have many names," he said. "But you may call me Urien."

"I'm Susannah," said Susannah. "This is Danielle."

"Lovely names. Susannah. Danielle." Urien made both names sound like something magical. "Tell me, how may I help you? For whom do you search? Do you seek a dream?"

"No," Susannah said. "A boy."

"Any boy? Or one particular boy?"

Danny's fists were clenched. She said, "Susannah, stop talking to him!"

"But he might know—" Susannah began.

"I don't care what he knows. I don't think he's human. I think he's a dream person and I don't trust him."

Urien smiled. Susannah gazed at him. I think he's human, she thought stubbornly. But she wasn't sure. Should she just go up to him and touch him with the stone? Surreptitiously she cupped it in her hand and pointed it in his direction. "We're looking for a human boy, not a dream boy," she said.

Urien shook his head. "No child from the mortal world lives here. This is Dreamland." A soft murmur arose at his back. *"Dreamland, Dreamland, yes."* The dreamfolk had gathered behind him to stare at them.

"He is here," Susannah said. "We saw him."

Urien's musical voice was doubtful. "How could you see into the Hill, little mortal?"

"In—" Susannah stopped. She had been about to answer, in Mother Bea's magic mirror. But if Urien were a dream person it

78

might not be a good idea to tell him that. "Never mind. We did. Do you mind if we look for him?"

As she said it, Susannah glanced at the stone.

It had changed! It was no longer gray. Instead, it had turned a shifting, cloudy white.

"Look away. But you will find only dreams in this place. Our empress, alas, is gone from home. Were she here I would lead you to her. You could tell her what you seek. She is very wise, and nothing happens in the dreamworld that she does not see. You should stay until she returns." He bowed and glided away.

Susannah thought miserably, He walks like a dream person. Mutely she held the stone out to show Danielle.

Danny stood with one hand on the butt of the ice axe. Her mouth was grim. "You told him too much," she said.

Susannah's stomach ached. "Maybe it won't matter."

"I hope not! Next time, you use that magic the witch gave us right away!" She put her hands on her hips. "Okay, let's find Niall. The *estupido*!" She frowned. "Where do we start to look? This is a big place."

"I don't know," Susannah said.

"Why don't you know? You're supposed to know about stories. I don't. What if the witch comes back and finds us here?"

"I don't know!"

"What if we find Niall and he doesn't want to come back?"

Susannah shivered. "Don't say that!"

She tried to tell herself that nothing bad happened to people in Adventures. But she was no longer sure of that. Her eyes prickled, and her chest hurt. She imagined herself going back home— somehow—and telling Mother and Daddy that Niall was in Dreamland. We went to the park and jumped through the moon. They would think she was just telling a story! They would be angry. They would call her crazy, and lock her up. They would call the police to look for Niall. When he didn't come back they would think that he was dead.

What if she never got home? Maybe the stories were wrong. Maybe the adventurers didn't always get out of Storyland . . .

"Hey!" Danielle said. She put both hands on Susannah's shoulders. Her fingers were strong and warm. "Susannah, I'm sorry I yelled at you. Please don't cry. I'm sorry."

Susannah swallowed. "But what if—"

"Don't," Danielle said. "I'm stupid, too." She touched Susannah's cheek. "Come on. Let's walk." She put her arm through Susannah's and pulled. Susannah sniffed back her tears.

"Where are we going?"

"To that big icicle." Danny pointed to a massive spike which hung from the ceiling. "We can start there, and walk outward in a big circle." She drew a spiral with one finger in the air.

"You think this is the only cave under the Hill?" Susannah said. "I bet there are more. Hundreds."

"Maybe there are more. But we have to start somewhere." Danny was stern. "Come on. We have to try." She walked toward the big icicle. A tiger with long curving fangs strolled from between two ice trees. They stopped and waited for it to leave their path.

"Psst!"

The girls jumped apart. Susannah turned to look behind them. No one was there.

Danny said, "I heard something. I know I did."

"Me too."

"Psst! Down here!"

They looked down.

A boy—not Niall—was crouching by the base of one of the tree-like pillars.

Jeanne Gomoll

Chapter Eight

He was pale, pale as one of the dreamfolk, but his eyes were a bright, bright blue. They glittered as the jewels in the painted tunnel had glittered.

He beckoned with both hands. Susannah started to kneel. Danny grabbed her arm. "Who are you?" she said.

"Not so loud." The boy made shushing motions. "They'll hear."

But none of the dreamfolk even looked in their direction. Danny released Susannah's arm. The boy wore a fancy costume of pale satin and lace. The clothes hung awkwardly on him.

"You're from outside, aren't you," he whispered. "You must be. You aren't faded."

"Who are you?" Danny repeated.

"I'm Francis."

"Are you from outside?" Susannah asked.

"I was." Glancing nervously about, he straightened up. He was taller than Susannah. "I've been here a long time. When I came I thought I was following my mother. But it was the Dreamkeeper, walking in the moonlight. She called to me—" he shook his head. "She was so beautiful. How did you come here?"

"We followed my brother," Susannah said. "He rode the Silver Horse through the moon."

Francis nodded. "The Horse was gone, I know. But it came back a while ago."

Danny said, "But it was tonight."

The blue-eyed boy shrugged. "Perhaps it was. There's no day or night under the Hill, only a shifting of the twilight. And dream time is different from the time outside."

Danny said suspiciously, "You claim you aren't a dream. You look like them."

"I know." Francis's voice was mournful. He held out his arms theatrically and stared at them. "Sometimes I wonder if I am wrong. Sometimes I think that I am a dream, the dream of a little boy named Francis Murray who went looking for his dead mother ome cool May evening." His voice grew singsong as if he were reciting a poem. "I have lingered too long in this enchanted world. I have become a dream, a shadow of the child I was, a ghost of the man I would have been." He held his hands in front of him. They were shaking. "Look, I have no more color than a ghost!"

He doesn't talk like a kid, Susannah thought. He talks like a grown-up. She squinted. It seemed to her that there were two people standing by the ice tree: a pale boy dressed in satin and lace and a tall man with blue eyes and red hair.

"Susannah!" Danny said. "Use the stone."

Quickly Susannah grabbed the lucky stone. She pressed it against Francis's outstretched arm.

Nothing happened. It did not change. "What is that?" Francis said.

"It's magic," Danny answered. "A witch gave it to us. If you had been a dream person, it would have changed color."

Francis's blue eyes blazed. "You have magic?"

Susannah was embarrassed. "Not exactly."

"Of course you have magic! Will you take me with you when you leave?" He caught her hand. "Christ! To leave this place, to see grass and trees, to hear birds and smell a new-mown field and feel the night wind on my face—" He stopped. His face twisted as if he were going to cry. "I am sorry," he whispered. "I have dreamed of this for so long—"

Danny said, "I bet dream people don't dream."

Susannah asked, "Have you tried to leave? Do they stop you?"

"I tried to leave once. It's hard to find the way. I got as far as the painted tunnel, but the colors hurt my eyes. And there are the harpies—" He bit his lip. "Perhaps I have been too long in the dreamworld, and cannot leave. In the real world I would be a ghost."

"What are harpies?" Susannah asked. But Francis did not hear her.

"Stop talking about ghosts!" Danny said impatiently. She closed strong fingers around Francis's forearm. Her hand was very dark against his pale skin. "Can you feel that?"

"Yes."

"Then you're not a ghost. If you were a ghost my fingers would go through you. Ghosts aren't solid."

"But what if I am a ghost outside?"

"Even if you are," Danny said, "wouldn't you rather be a ghost outside than a prisoner here? You don't belong here."

Francis rubbed his face with the side of his hand. "Yes. You are right. But I've been here so long. I don't remember the world beyond the Hill. Everything will have changed. My father must be dead by now. Perhaps you know of him? Thomas Murray of county Kinross. He's an under-sheriff."

Susannah looked at Danielle, who shrugged. "We're from San Francisco," Susannah said. "My father drives a bus."

"A bus?" Francis frowned. "I don't know what that is."

"Wow!" said Danny. "You've been here a long time."

How long? Susannah wondered. A hundred years? More?

Danny said, "You really want to leave?"

Francis squared his shoulders. "Yes. I do."

"Then we'll help you. We can lead you through the painted tunnel." She looked at Susannah. "Right?" Susannah nodded. "But you have to help us find Niall, Susannah's brother. This is Susannah."

"Hello," Susannah said. Francis put his right hand over his heart and bowed. She curtsyed.

"I'm Danny. Now, you said you'd seen the Silver Horse come back from outside awhile ago. Was there a small boy riding him?"

"I did not see one," Francis said. "But that does not mean there was no boy. What does he look like, this boy?"

"This tall." Susannah held her hand palm down to show how tall Niall was. "His eyes are blue, like yours but not so bright. His hair's yellow, and it curls. And his ears stick out from his head." She pushed her own ears forward to show how Niall's ears jutted through his hair. "He was wearing his pajamas with the horses on them."

"Pa-ja-mas," repeated Francis. "What's that?"

"Clothes to wear to sleep."

"A nightshirt?"

"Sort of. With pictures of horses' heads on it. Blue."

Francis waved a hand at the white walls. His voice grew singsong. "After a time in the dreamworld all things fade."

Susannah shivered. She imagined herself and Danny hunting through the cracks and crannies of the icy cavern, looking for a little boy grown pale as the walls. But Niall had not been *that* long in the dreamworld. Neither she nor Danielle had faded—had they? She stared with terror at Danielle's glossy black curls.

"What's the matter with you?" Danny said.

No, they hadn't faded, not one bit. Angry at herself for permitting Francis to scare her, Susannah said, "Nothing. I was thinking about Niall. I'm sure we can find him!"

"All *right!*" said Danielle.

Francis flushed. It brought real color to his pale cheeks and made him look less like a dream person. "You have spirit," he said. "Where have you looked for Niall?"

"We were going to start at that big icicle," said Danny.

A dark shadow glided over them. A horrible, harsh voice screamed. Francis ducked. Shrilly he cried, "The harpies! Run! Hide!" He scrambled for the shelter of a crevice.

Susannah looked up.

Three huge birds with leathery wings and human faces soared overhead. Blood dripped from their mouths through dagger-like fangs. Their edged claws reached for her. They stank, of old shoes and dead things and rooms that had been opened once and never again.

Susannah crawled to the wall. The harpies' wings flapped, sending the heavy smell toward her. They croaked at her derisively. Go away! Susannah wanted to call to them. This isn't *your* story.

But maybe it wasn't her story either. Shivering, she remembered the bones in the painted tunnel. Had the harpies killed him? There were stories in which the hero was killed and the monster won.

What if this were one of them?

The harpies gnashed their jaws together. Their wings beat. They hovered nearer. Susannah hid her head under her arms.

"Go away!" said an angry voice. "Get out! Go!"

Susannah lifted her head from her arms.

Danielle knelt at her feet. She was holding the ice axe in both hands. Its bird head pointed toward them. The blade was burning. "Get out!" she said, and stood. Susannah could see her legs shaking.

The middle harpy screamed. Her foul breath eddied around them. Susannah almost choked. It tasted of burning tires. There were tears on Danny's cheeks, but she stayed on her feet, holding the burning ice axe out. The harpies screamed, and circled, but they came no closer.

At last, with slow beats of their ponderous wings, they soared away.

Susannah waited. And waited. Her elbow stung. She had skinned it. The harpies did not come back. Finally she stood. Her knees were shaking. "Danny. That was wonderful." Her voice came out a croak.

Danny still held the ice axe in both hands. The blade had stopped burning. "It worked," Danny said. "I didn't think it would." She lifted the axe. "Did you see it? It was on fire!" She sagged against the wall. "Oh, wow. I was scared."

"Yeah." Susannah gazed across the cavern. Would the harpies come back now? Her stomach hurt to think about them. "You were really brave."

"I didn't know what else to do." Danielle slid the axe into its loop. "If I hadn't had this—I wonder what they would have done to us."

"Eaten us!" said Francis, levering himself out of the crack in which he had hidden.

"What?"

"Yes." Francis nodded. "They eat humans. They are terrible." He bowed to Danny. "You were brave, lady. You saved us."

Danny shook her head. "The axe saved us."

"What if they find my brother?" Susannah said. "He's only a little boy. Will they eat him?"

"They might if they could," Francis said. "But the Silver Horse brought him here; he is under the Dreamlady's protection. She'll be kind to him until he wearies her."

His voice was bitter. Danielle said, "She was nice to you once, huh?" Francis nodded. "God, what a freaky place this is. We better find Niall and get out of here. I don't think I want any more adventures."

Susannah rubbed her arms. She was cold. The shadowless light hurt her eyes and made her squint. Her elbow stung. "How did they find us?" she asked.

"They smelled you," Francis said. "You smell warm."

"Oh yeah?" Danny said. "How come they don't eat you?"

"I don't smell warm," Francis said sadly. "I've been here too long. I smell like one of the dreamfolk."

"Oh." She gazed across the cavern. "I thought maybe that man sent them."

"What man?"

"He had a sword. He spoke to us just before we met you. Urien."

"Urien! You met him?" Francis frowned. "He is dangerous. He is the Dreamlady's consort. Most of the dreamfolk have no life, save what she gives them. But Urien moves and speaks on his own."

"Can he call the harpies?" Susannah asked.

"I don't know."

"Will he stop us from getting to Niall?"

"He may try. Or he may laugh and not care. The dreamfolk are very fickle." He beckoned. "Come."

"Where?" said Danielle.

Francis put a finger across his lips. "We'll speak with the magician. He's not one of the dreamfolk. He lives in a tree, and he knows everything that happens in the dreamworld—maybe everything that happens everywhere. He will know where your brother is."

Susannah's heart thumped. "Will he tell us?"

"If he won't, no one else can."

Danny grew defiant. "If he won't, we'll look. We'll find Niall ourselves!"

Quietly they crept across the vast white cavern. Susannah blew on her hands. It seemed to her that the air was growing colder. She wondered what that meant. Francis led them on a twisting, turning path. The dreamfolk watched them, smiling vague smiles, but no one spoke to them or tried to stop or delay them.

Just when Susannah was sure he was lost, he halted by a huge ice tree. It was colorless, but if it had not been, Susannah thought, it would have been a redwood. Its trunk was big as a small house, and it went up and up until its branches disappeared into the cavern's roof.

Danielle knocked on the trunk, *thunk*. It was a solid sound. "I thought you said this tree was hollow," she said.

"I never said that," Francis answered.

"You said the magician lived in the tree!"

"He does. You are standing too close to see him. Step back."

Both girls stepped back. "I don't see anything," Danielle complained. "I see a big tree, just bark and leaves and—oh wow!" Her fingers gripped Susannah's forearm. "Susannah, look."

A face was gazing at them out of the tree trunk.

It was a man's face. Squinting, Susannah put a hand up, shading her eyes. At first she thought the eyes, nose, mouth and bushy beard were a pattern in the seemingly transparent bark, but then she saw that the face connected to a neck, the neck to shoulders and chest. . . . Out of the tree, the man would be a giant. He filled the trunk. His feet were planted against the icy floor of the cave; his arms were branches lifted to the icicles. Susannah could not tell where the tree stopped and the man began.

Danielle whispered, "Does he ever come out?"

"No. He's been here a long time. The Dreamlady put him here, it's said. Once he was the most powerful wizard in the world, but he grew old and tired. Mostly he sleeps and dreams. When he isn't sleeping, he watches." Francis put his mouth against the bark. "Magician, wake!"

A deep whisper flowed from the tree. "I am awake, Francis. Good day."

He had a green voice, Susannah decided. Some voices came in colors. Her mother's voice was pale blue. Danielle's was red. Celie's was a bright, hot purple. She stepped back farther. The wizard's skin was gnarled like tree bark. His long hair and beard seemed to be part of the tree. His eyes were half open. They gleamed a pale green—like new uncurling leaves—beneath his drooping lids.

I could draw him, Susannah thought. She clenched her fists. She wanted her paint box and brush and paper so badly that she felt *squeezed*.

"Good day, Susannah. Good day, Danielle," the green voice said.

Danny gasped. "He knows our names!"

"I told you," Francis said. "He knows everything. Magician, there is a little boy here, come from the world outside. He has yellow hair and blue eyes. He came riding the Silver Horse. His sister and her friend desire to rescue him. Can you see him?"

Susannah held her breath.

"I see him," the magician said. "He sits dreaming at the foot of the empress's throne. An orange cat is with him."

"Mr. D!" exclaimed Danielle. She grinned. "Well. I guess he is a magic cat."

Susannah let her breath out. Stepping forward, she pressed her palm against the pale bark. It was *warm*. "Thank you," she said to the magician.

"You are welcome, Susannah," said the green voice.

"We better get moving," Danny said. She hugged herself. "It's getting colder in here. Where's the empress's what-he-said?"

"Throne," Francis said. He pointed across the cavern. "See that big icicle?" It was the one they had noticed. "They call it the Sword. The Dreamkeeper's throne sits beneath it."

"Great. Let's go."

"Wait. Please." Francis turned back to the tree. "Magician, I am going with them to the outside world. Wish me godspeed."

"I do, Francis." The magician sighed. The pale leaves rustled. "I am sorry you must go. It has been pleasant to hear a young voice now and again, over the years."

"Magician—" Francis stopped. "Magician, if I leave the Hill, will I be a ghost?"

The wizard laughed. The tree branches swayed. The green eyes opened wider. "No, Francis, you will not be a ghost. But you will not be a little boy, either."

"I am glad," Francis said. His voice seemed to have gotten strangely deep. "Thank you, Magician."

Questions bubbled in Susannah's head. *Are you real? Do you really know everything? How come you can't get out of Dreamland?* The giant's eyes were closing. *When you sleep, what do you dream? Are you dreaming this? Are you dreaming ME?*

The giant's eyes were shut. A murmur—his breathing—filled the cavern.

Slowly the three children made their way across the cavern to the Dreamlady's throne. Danielle and Susannah were shivering. Francis, despite his flimsy clothes, did not seem cold. "Hurry," he muttered. "We must hurry." He kept looking behind him.

The throne was huge. A long flight of steep steps approached it. The Sword hung over it, its tip needle-sharp. The throne gleamed. It was big enough for a giant to sit on. It looked as if it had been carved from a block of ice.

93

Danny shaded her face with her hands. "I don't see him." Then she yelled. "There he is!"

Susannah peeked through her fingers. She saw a blob of orange. "Mr. D!" she shouted.

She ran to him.

The big cat switched his tail. He looked fat and tough and pleased with himself. "You smarty," Susannah said. "Where's Niall?"

"Meow," said the cat. He bounded up the steps, tail waving like a kite string. Four, five, six—on the seventh step he halted.

On the step above him sat a little boy in blue pajamas.

"Niall!" Susannah hollered. Leaping to the eighth step, she knelt beside her brother. "Niall, come on!"

Niall looked at her with wide, vacant eyes as if he had never seen her before. Politely, like a child meeting a stranger, he backed away from her, ducked his head shyly, and smiled.

Jeanne Gomoll

Chapter Nine

            "He doesn't know you," Francis called. "He's been enchanted. There's a spell on him. He doesn't recognize you."

Susannah looked into Niall's eyes. They were dead as the painted eyes of the broken dolls. "Niall!"

Danny leaped up the steps. Francis followed her. "What's wrong?"

Susannah said, "He doesn't know who I am!" Her nose itched. Crying won't help! she told herself. She rubbed it vigorously.

Danny scowled. "That's silly. He's playing. Niall, we're going home." She reached to grab him.

"So," said a lazy voice, "you have found the boy you were searching for! Greetings again, mortals." It was Urien. He smiled at them from the lowest step. His elegant silks seemed to glimmer. "Susannah, Danielle, Francis—" he purred their names. Francis moaned. "And Niall. Who rode the Silver Horse into the Hill and stayed to dream lovely dreams."

"Niall," Danny said, "you better come with us."

Niall looked at her without recognition.

"It seems he does not want to go with you, Danielle." Urien smiled. His left hand gripped the hilt of his sword. "A pity. You came all the way from the far world to find him. But your journey need not be in vain. Perhaps you should stay with us too." He looked at Susannah, and his smile grew. "There are many fine adventures in Dreamland."

Susannah shook her head. "We can't stay. We have to go home. My mother and father will worry." She turned urgently to Niall. "Niall, we have to go back to Allan Street. Mother and Daddy are waiting for us. Don't you want to play in the park and eat fried chicken and chocolate cake and ride on Daddy's bus?"

Memory struggled with magic in Niall's vacant eyes. "Bus?"

"Yes! Remember the red and yellow bus that Daddy drives? I made you a picture of it. Remember the park on Allan Street, with the swings and the slide? Remember Mr. D? Look, he's right here. He came with us to find you." The cat's tail lashed. "Remember tacos and ice cream, and going to the beach? Remember Celie and Juanito?"

"Quiet!" Urien called. "Dreamfolk, assemble! I command you!"

"Remember the street fair? You were a clown. Mother played the tambourine."

"Mother," Niall said. He rubbed his eyes. The blank look had left them. "Susannah?" He looked around. "Susannah, I'm cold."

He was whining. Susannah didn't care. He knew her! Grabbing him, she pulled him close, hugging him hard. He did not struggle from her. "Niall, we're going home."

"Hurry," Francis said, "oh, hurry. They're watching us!" Below them Urien stood, hand on his sword, his pale face stern. Behind him the dreamfolk were gathering. They glided languorously across the icy floor, barely interested, but there.

Susannah took Niall's hand. "Come on, Niall. Let's go. Danny?"

"Yeah," Danielle said, "I'm here."

"Francis? We're going down the steps *now*."

"Yes," Francis whispered. "Yes, we must." He stood beside her. Danny moved to stand beside Niall. "The door is there." He pointed across the cavern.

Susannah stepped down a step. Another step. Another. Six. Five. Four. Three. Two. They reached the last step. "Stop," Urien said.

He drew his sword. Around, behind him, the dreamfolk drifted. "Stop. You cannot pass."

It was colder. A wind blew through the Hill. Susannah shivered. She made her voice strong. "You can't keep us if we don't want to stay."

"Who told you that?" said Urien. His smile was cruel. "It's wrong. We can keep you. Feel. It is growing colder. Soon it will grow very cold. You will sleep. When you wake you will have forgotten what you came to do, forgotten the world outside, forgotten all thoughts of leaving. You will no longer be cold. Don't struggle. Why not choose to stay? You will not be unhappy. No one is unhappy in the dreamworld."

It was very cold. Danielle was shivering. Niall's teeth were chattering. Susannah felt as if her feet were frozen to the floor.

What, she thought dazedly, if Urien spoke truth; what if they could not leave?

But they had to leave. They had to.

"Danny," she said.

"Wha—" Danny looked slowly around.

"Your ice axe. Take it out!"

"Um?" Danny's hands moved to her belt. She seemed to snap awake. "Oh, yeah!"

"Francis!" Susannah made her voice crackle, like Mr. Gonzalez did when he was serious about being listened to. "Hold Niall's hand!"

Francis extended his left hand to Niall. He was trembling. "They'll stop us," he said.

"They won't. Niall, squeeze my hand. Danny, you ready?"

"Ready!" Holding the ice axe in both hands, Danny lifted it and pointed it at Urien.

He raised his sword.

Light gathered on the edge of Danny's axe. It sprang at Urien. A wind howled around their ears. Mr. D. stalked forward, tail lashing. He was swollen to twice his normal size. The dreamfolk muttered. Danny swung the blazing axe at Urien. The swordsman slid back. She swung again. He backed away from her. She leaped at him.

"Yaaah!" Danny yelled. She swung the axe at Urien's sword. It struck. The sword shivered—and cracked, into a thousand shards of ice. They fell to the cavern's floor. Danny's feet crunched on the icy bits.

Susannah cheered. "Way to go!"

"Nyaa nyaa, I'll break you too!" Danny jeered at Urien. "They can't stop us now! Francis! Where's that door?" Francis, freed, burst forward through the crowd of dreamfolk. Danny followed, brandishing the burning axe. They brushed Urien aside. Susannah ran after her, dragging Niall by the hand.

They were almost to the door when great gobbling laughter filled their ears. Huge winged shadows swooped over them.

Francis cried out. "The harpies!" Falling to his knees, he covered his head with his arms.

"Go!" Danny shouted, gesturing at the archway to the painted tunnel. "I'll hold them off." She stepped away from the door and pointed the axe at the harpies.

Susannah pushed Niall through the archway. The terrible smell made her want to throw up. Danny held the ice axe in both hands. It burned and burned. The frustrated harpies screamed at her and flexed their talons.

"Francis, come on!" Susannah yelled.

"I can't," he sobbed, "I can't."

"Crawl!"

He started to crawl—in the wrong direction! He was crawling back into the cavern.

"No," Susannah shouted, "this way!" He did not seem to hear her. The smallest harpy giggled: a hideous sound. She began to sink slowly toward him.

"Damn!" Susannah whirled on Niall. "You stay there, you understand!" Wide-eyed, he nodded. Crouching like a runner, Susannah counted to herself: one, two, three, go! Charging past Danny, she lunged at Francis, pulled him up, and shoved him at the archway. "This way. Move!"

He stumbled forward. The hovering harpy stooped. Susannah felt a tearing pain across her back. Sobbing, she half fell. Danny grabbed her, pulling. Susannah forced her legs to work. Her back hurt. Warmth eddied about them. "We made it!" Danny yelled. Then her voice grew soft. "Susannah, are you all right? Your back—" her breath hissed.

"Is it bleeding?" Susannah said. Her back felt hot and cold all at once. Her legs shook. She leaned on the wall. Behind her Niall was crying.

"It's bleeding," Danny said behind her. "It looks pretty gross, but it's just one scratch, not very deep. You need a new shirt, though. Niall, shut up! You aren't hurt, Susannah is."

Susannah straightened. "I'm okay," she said. She made herself take a few steps. It wasn't so bad.

Francis was standing very still with a hand over his eyes.

"Francis, what's the matter?" Danny said.

"It hurts," he said. "The colors. So many colors."

"Keep your eyes shut," Danny said. "I'll lead you."

He groped forward with one hand. "Susannah," he said hoarsely, "thank you. You saved me."

Susannah did not know what to say. She felt embarrassed. "It's okay," she said. "No big deal."

The trip through the painted tunnel seemed much shorter than it had been the first time. Niall wanted to stop to watch the jewels flicker on the walls, but Susannah wouldn't let him. He whined constantly; she had to clench her fingers into fists to keep from smacking him. Her back stung. Danny led Francis by the wrist. Mr. D strolled ahead of them, tail sweeping from side to side. When they looked at him, he mewed.

"Come, Niall," Susannah coaxed. "We have to catch Mr. D."

They left the painted tunnel. In the lightless passage Francis, sighing with relief, opened his eyes. Niall started to sniffle. He was afraid of the dark.

"You baby, Niall," Danny fumed.

"He just wants to be carried," Susannah said. Her legs ached and her elbow stung and her back hurt. The bleeding had stopped, but her shirt was sticking to her back. If she bent too much it felt as if her skin was tearing off.

Francis said, "I can help. Let me. Niall, come walk with me up front. We will be the vanguard, see?" His voice floated back through the tunnel. "This is a pleasant game, isn't it? You are a big boy. How old are you now? Six. Six is old. Too big to cry."

Suddenly a shaft of light touched the rocks at their feet.

"Mommy!" Niall said. Sliding from Francis's arms, he ran

toward the light. With a sigh of relief and resentment, Susannah started to follow him. Stupid brat, she thought. He hadn't said thank you, not once.

Sliding forward, she bumped into Francis. "Go on," she said.

"I'm afraid," he whispered. "What if the magician was wrong? What if I am a ghost in the far world?"

"Too late!" Danny said. "You can't go back." Grabbing his wrist, she yanked. They popped from darkness into the thin evening sunlight.

"Grass," whispered Francis, "trees, birds, sunshine—" He closed his eyes and stretched out his arms. Mist coiled around his legs. The sunlight played across his face. Susannah's heart gave a panicked thump. She thought, What if he is a ghost? She imagined him fading or cracking into bits. But he did not fade, and he did not grow brittle and crack. He simply stood there, a tall red-haired boy on a twilit lawn, wearing funny clothes.

A voice called. "Susannah! Danny! Over here!"

The children turned. Sarah stood at the forest's edge. The trees loomed behind her. It's wonderful to see shadows, Susannah thought. "Hurry," Sarah called. "It's almost sundown!"

Wasn't there some reason, Susannah thought, why we had to come back before night?

She reached for Niall's hand.

The mist swirled between them. A cold wind blew across her path. Shivering, Susannah turned in a circle. The mist swept across her eyes. She couldn't see. She yelled. "Niall! Danny!"

"Susannah!"

"Children," sang a sweet voice, "where are you going?"

It was the Dreamlady. She smiled. She was beautiful, just as beautiful as she had looked in the mirror. Her hair was snowy. She wore a high glittering crown. The mist wrapped around her legs and shoulders and feet. She seemed to be floating in it. Behind her the Silver Horse reared and pranced, arched neck graceful, red eyes aflame. The strength drained from Susannah's tired legs. The mist—it was very soft, like a pillow—held her in its arms. Gently it pushed her back from the forest.

The Dreamlady stretched out her arms. "Susannah," she crooned, "stay. You need not be in such a hurry to leave my Hill. Here are all the stories you have ever wanted. You love adventure: I have Adventures aplenty in the dreamworld. You will never grow too old to play with them. They will be yours, yours alone. Niall will not disturb them. You will never have to go to school, or go to the store, or watch your baby brother. There are no baby brothers in the Hill. You will be the baby, the darling. Stay and dream, Susannah. Stay."

I must go home, Susannah thought. But she did not move. The mist had blotted Niall and Danny and Francis from sight. She was alone with the Lady. The mist felt warm. It pushed her at the Hill. She yielded to it one step, and stopped. Adventures were fun, but you could not have adventures all the time. Would there be a way for her to paint, in the dreamworld? It had no colors. Dreams would not stay solid long enough for her to paint; she had tried. It would not be fun to be alone under the Hill without her parents, without Danielle, without the streetcars and the park and the skyscrapers. She would even miss Niall, a little. . . .

She stuck her chin out. "I don't want to stay," she said firmly. "I want to go home."

The mist uncurled itself from her feet. She could move.

The Dreamlady was speaking. "Come with me, Danielle. Here in my Hill is the life you want. You will climb the mountains of dream, taller than Rainier, taller than Chomolungma. There will not be anything you cannot do."

"Danny!" Susannah yelled. "Don't listen to her!" She wondered if Danielle could hear her. "Danny, don't go with her, please!"

Danielle's voice came clearly through the mist. "No. I want to go home."

The Dreamlady held out her arms. Her voice grew sweeter, softer, more seductive. "Niall, stay with me. I want a little boy to play with, to hug and hold. You will not have to go to school. No one will make you go to bed, or take a bath. Susannah will not be there. There will be no new baby in the house. You will ride the Silver Horse whenever you like. He waits for you!"

"Horse?" Niall said.

The Silver Horse neighed. The Dreamlady smiled. Numbly Susannah wondered how she would explain to her mother where Niall was. . . . He would go. It was too hard for a six-year-old to resist that call.

"Mowr!" Mr. D came leaping through the mist with tiger grace.

Niall pushed his lower lip out, the way he did when Mother tried to coax him into doing something he didn't want to do. "No!" he said. "Don't want to. It's cold!"

"Cat-cat," whispered the Dreamlady, "will *you* come with me to the Dreamland?"

Mr. D stared at her contemptuously. Growling softly, he switched his tiger tail.

Rising, the Dreamlady let her arms fall. She laughed. "So none of you will stay with me. I have lost three children and a cat. And what of Francis, little Frank? Shall you depart the dreamworld, Francis Murray, now that you are little no longer? Much time has passed outside since you followed a white lady into the Hill. The world you go to is neither dreamworld nor the far world. You may not like it."

"No, Lady." Francis' voice was deep and firm. "I will stay in Dreamland no longer. The world has changed, but so have I." The mist blew back from him. He was tall, broad-shouldered; a young man with red hair and green eyes; a grown-up. With steady strides he crossed the green grass to Niall and lifted the little boy in his arms.

"Go then," said the Dreamlady. Her laugh rang like bells. "But think of me, children, when the moonlight shines and you wake, troubled, from sleep. Think of me in the bright day when your dreams desert you and the clamor of the world crowds your mind.

103

Think of me. Remember the Hill of Dreams!" Mist leaped about her like gray flame. Then she was gone.

The setting sun spread across the green. The travelers stretched, looking about them with wide eyes.

A slim, gray-clad girl was waving to them from the other side of the lawn.

Chapter Ten

"Sarah!" shouted Danielle. She loped across the lawn.

Francis set Niall on his feet again. His blue eyes were dreamy. Kneeling, he brushed the grass with his palms.

Niall started to follow Danny. Susannah grabbed him, wincing as her shirt pulled at the skin on her back. "Stupid brat," she said. "I'm not going to lose you again. You walk with me." She marched him toward Sarah, one hand locked tightly in the collar of his pajama top. It's over, she thought; our Adventure's over. But she did not feel sad. They had done it: they had rescued Niall from the Hill. More than Niall . . . . She glanced at Francis. He was staring at the trees, his head tipped back. He looked wholly like a grown-up. She wondered what it would be like to turn from a kid into a grown-up in one second.

Sarah's smile was spread across her whole face. "I saw you in the mirror when you came out to the lawn. Mother Bea sent me to meet you. I was terrified when the Dreamkeeper appeared! I heard everything she said to you. I tried to call you but the mist blew my words away. But you were so courageous, so strong!" She beamed at them. "This is Niall? Hello, Niall."

Niall leaned against Susannah and mumbled.

"And who is the tall man who came through the door with you?"

"His name's Francis," Danny said. "He was a little boy in the Hill." Francis saw them looking at him. Crossing the grass, he came to stand beside them. "This is Sarah. She's learning to be a witch."

The two of them gazed at each other for a long moment. Francis said, "Good day, lady. I have never met a student witch before."

Sarah smiled. "Were you truly a child in the Hill?"

"I was. And despite the Dreamlady's words to me, this world does not seem to have changed much. Only I have."

"But this is not the world you left," Sarah said.

"Is it not? But I see grass and the sun and a pine forest, and a pretty woman in a dove-gray gown."

Sarah's cheeks flushed red. "Nevertheless it is not the world you left. That was the human world. This world is Storyland." Her gentle voice grew severe. "And you should not say such things to an apprentice witch."

"I beg pardon," Francis said. He bowed. "Shall I now be turned

106

into a toad? I hope not. I am just growing accustomed to this form. I was taught to be truthful. I have not unlearned it in the dreamworld."

A gust of wind rushed through the pine trees. Niall whined, "Susannah, I'm cold."

"Don't whine," Susannah said. But the sunlight was almost gone. Niall's pajamas were thin.

"Come," Sarah said, "we'll go to the house." She turned to lead them to it.

Niall dragged his feet. "Susannah, carry me."

"No," Susannah said wearily, "I can't, Niall. My back hurts." Sarah heard. "Why does your back pain you?" she asked.

"The harpies scratched her," Danny said.

Francis added softly, "She was very brave. She saved my life."

"Let me see." Susannah turned her back so that Sarah could look at it. "Ah. Here." A wonderful coolness spread across Susannah's back. "Is that better?"

Susannah swung her arms. She worked her shoulders. It did not hurt. "Thank you."

The witch's house was welcoming in the gray twilight. Light streamed from the front windows. The front door opened by itself as they reached it. "Well, come in!" Francis jumped. "Thought you'd never get here. Took you long enough!"

Sarah ushered them into the room with the cauldron. Mother Bea stood beside it, leaning on her cane. She smiled at them. "So," she said, "the adventurers are back."

Niall stared at her. His mouth grew round. Susannah patted his shoulder. "Say hello," she prompted.

He whispered it. "Hello."

"Welcome to my house, Niall. I am Mother Bea. Are you still cold? You may step closer to the fire to get warm."

"Meow!" said Mr. D. He jumped to the table top. Tail erect, head cocked at its haughtiest angle, he advanced upon the witch.

"Good evening, cousin. I know what you want." Mother Bea

pointed a bony finger. A saucer floated through the air and landed on the table. There was milk in it. Purring, the cat crouched. His tongue flicked the milk.

"Sit!" said the witch.

Susannah sank thankfully into the blue armchair. Danielle sat in the red one. Niall climbed into Susannah's lap.

"And who," said the witch, "is the stranger with you?"

Francis was still standing in the doorway. At the witch's question, he bowed. "Francis Murray is my name, madam. I am—I *was*—a child of the far world. I was eleven when I followed the Dreamkeeper into the Hill, thinking she was my dead mother returned to me. And now—" he held out his arms—"how old am I? I cannot tell."

Mother Bea nodded. "Two hundred years have passed since you entered Dreamland, Francis Murray. Your home is gone, your family scattered."

He swallowed. The freckles stood out on his cheeks. "Two hundred years. That is a long time." He passed a hand across his face. "The world must be much changed. Will it have a place in it for me?"

"No," said the witch gently. "Too much time has passed. It is too late."

"Perhaps I should return to the dreamworld."

"You cannot. That door will not admit you."

"Then where may I go?" he asked.

Mother Bea looked at him a long moment. "You may stay here."

Sarah started. She fiddled with the folds of her gown. Francis looked at her. A smile flickered across his face. "It seems a pleasant haven," he said. "Where and what is it?"

"It is as Sarah told you: it is Storyland. It is larger than this small corner would suggest. There are places in it not unlike the world you left. I think you will contrive to be content."

"I will try to do so," Francis said. He looked at Sarah.

"Sarah," Mother Bea said, "show Francis where he is to sleep."

"Yes, Mother Bea. Will you follow me, then?" she said to the red-haired man. The two of them went into the hall. Danielle made a face and mouthed a silent word. It looked, Susannah thought, like 'mushy.'

A chuckle floated from the corner of the ceiling. Anansi said, "You shall have to call an imp to watch your fire for you, sister."

"For a little while," said Mother Bea. She looked at the children. "And now, what shall we do with you three? In your world the full moon rides low over the sea. It's time for you to be gone. Danielle, put the ice axe on the table."

"Must I?" Danny said.

"Yes."

Reluctantly, Danny rose from the chair, took off the belt, and laid it and the ice axe on top of the table. Mother Bea pointed at the axe and belt and spoke. The room darkened. Susannah tightened her arms around Niall.

His head slipped against her shoulder. Softly, he snored.

The light returned. A pocket knife and four prosaic, dirty pieces of string lay on the table. Picking them up, Danny pushed them into her pocket. Susannah found the thong of the lucky stone and pulled it over her head.

"Here," she said to Danielle, "it's yours. You take it."

Danny closed her fingers around it. Susannah glanced at Mother Bea, wondering if there was something that had to be done to make the stone stop being magic. Mother Bea did not seem to notice. It had helped a lot, Susannah thought, to have the magic things with them. In the painted tunnel she had—she had—what had she done? She felt bits and pieces of the adventure slipping from her memory.

"But it just happened!" she cried. "I don't want to forget it!"

"What?" Danny looked at her oddly.

Mother Bea said, "You will not forget what you need to remember, Susannah."

The magician, Susannah thought, I must remember the magician, and this house. And the talking door. And the skeleton in the painted tunnel.

"Stand up," Mother Bea said to her. "Let me have your shirt." Carefully—she did not want to wake him—Susannah slid Niall to the seat of the chair. She pulled her shirt over her head. A rip gaped from the left shoulder across to the bottom edge of the right side hem. She remembered the stench of the harpies, and their terrible laughter. She shuddered.

"Give it to me."

Susannah gave her shirt to the witch. Holding it by one of the sleeves, Mother Bea slowly dipped it in the cauldron. Susannah stared as it came out of the pot. It was dry. The witch held it out to her. She took it. It was whole, with no sign of where the rip had been. She put it on. The fabric seemed thicker, softer.

"Now," Mother Bea said, "we must walk. The gate through which you entered Storyland is still open. I will close it behind you when you leave. There will be no more adventurers in Storyland tonight!"

Danielle yawned, and knuckled her eyes. Curled in the chair, Niall yawned and mumbled in his sleep. Susannah yawned. "Are we going far?" she asked. "Niall's very tired." She wished they did not have to leave at once. It would be neat to sleep one night in a witch's house.

She gazed around the room, not wanting to forget a thing. That pitcher was the djinn's lamp. That transparent dangly thing was the skin of a worm whose name she couldn't remember.

"Susannah's tired, too," commented the spider.

Suddenly Francis and Sarah entered the room. Francis lifted Niall from the chair. Susannah blinked at him. "I thought you were staying here."

"I am. But I will go with you as far as the gate." He smiled at her, a grown-up smile. Susannah felt shy of him.

Niall wound his arms around Francis's neck. "Daddy," he murmured.

"Here I come," said the spider. The spider web shivered. Then the spider descended from the corner, dropping at the end of a fragile silver thread. She landed on Mother Bea's collar. The witch reeled the thread in. Susannah could not see what happened to it. She could barely see the spider, black against the black of Mother Bea's clothes.

"Let us go," said the witch.

The front door opened without anyone touching it.

Danny giggled. "I wish our door could do that." They stepped onto the porch. Susannah felt for Danny's hand. She was not scared, exactly—but the pine trees outside the house were very tall, and it was dark.

The door closed. "Good-bye," it said.

"Good-bye," the children said.

"Until we meet again," the door said. It had a mouth now, and two eyes. One of the eyes closed in a long wink. Susannah grinned.

Walking toward the trees, Mother Bea held her staff out. The eyes of the wooden bird on the head began to glow. The light showed a path covered with pine needles. The pine needles were slippery; Susannah gripped Danny's hand. The broken dolls were here somewhere, she thought. But they wouldn't bother Mother Bea; Susannah was sure of that.

She felt a warm tail stroke her knee. "Hello, cat," she said. Danny was shivering. "Hey. You cold?"

"Yeah. Aren't you?"

"No."

"We are almost there," Anansi said.

A cricket called, *chuckahchuckahchuckahchuck!* A wind rattled the sentinel pines. Then, suddenly, they were out of the woods. Ahead of them stretched a dark plain. The sky was brilliant with a million stars.

"Where are we?" Danny said.

"In the grasslands," said the witch. "This is where Susannah landed when she jumped through the moon." She pointed with the staff. "There is the tree you slept beneath, Susannah. We must go to it. Can you see it?"

Susannah squinted. "No."

Francis said softly, "Where is the moon?"

"Behind us," said Mother Bea. "It is hidden by the trees. Soon it will set. The light on the horizon is the light of the rising sun."

What light? Susannah thought. She squinted at the horizon. Crickets called, and then a bird, and another and another. . . . Overhead the stars burned.

She saw—not light—a lessening of the darkness.

They walked through the tall grass. The light grew. Susannah gazed ahead. There was something on the horizon: she supposed it was the tree. The stars seemed dimmer and smaller. Soon they would be gone. Mr. Gonzalez had said they didn't really go anywhere, you just couldn't see them because the sunlight was so bright, like a flashlight in a sunny room.

Maybe magic is like that, Susannah thought. Maybe it's always present, but hard to see unless you knew where to find it.

"What's that?" Danielle said. "Look out! It's a bear!"

"Murgatroyd!" Susannah said. "It's all right. It's friendly. It knows me." She ran forward toward the big brown beast. "Hello, Mug."

The bear blinked. "Hello. Ah. Hello. Oh, it's you. You're back." It yawned. "Did you find the girl? Or was it a boy—"

"I found him," Susannah said. "I found my friend Danny too, in the woods. We found Mother Bea like Aloysius said, and then we went into the Hill and found Niall and Francis, and we left. We're going home."

"Oh," said the bear. It rocked back and forth. "Are all these people going with you?"

"No. Mother Bea and Sarah and Francis are staying here. But Danny and Niall and I are going back. And Mr. D, of course."

The bear's deep voice was plaintive. "Must you leave?"

"Yes."

"I suppose you won't come back."

"Probably not."

The bear nodded. "I thought you wouldn't." It looked very sad. It dropped to all fours. Susannah reached to stroke its soft muzzle.

"I wish you wouldn't look like that," she said.

"What's the matter with him?" Danny asked, coming up to Susannah's elbow.

"He's a grown-up teddy bear and he's sad because nobody here will play with him. The elephants don't like to play and the monkey—the gibbon, I mean—is really snotty."

"How do you know this?"

"I told you. I met him when I woke up. He carried me to the jungle. We ate bananas."

"Yeah?" Danny walked respectfully around the bear. "He's really big, you know."

Niall woke suddenly from his sleep. He gazed at the bear and chuckled. Wriggling from Francis's grip, he ran across the grass to Murgatroyd and reached fearlessly to pat the bear's fur. "Hello, bear."

"Hello," said Murgatroyd. "Are you a boy or a girl?"

"I'm Niall."

"Ah. Ah. My name is Mug."

Susannah felt a stab of jealous anger. "Niall, leave the bear alone," she said. "We have to go to the tree."

Niall ignored her. She looked at Mother Bea for help.

Danny said thoughtfully, "I bet he could come with us. I bet Mother Bea could magic him. He could live in the zoo with the other bears."

"Maybe," Susannah said, watching Niall stroke Murgatroyd's button nose. "Mother Bea, could you turn Murgatroyd into a real bear?"

Mother Bea said, "Murgatroyd, would you want to be a real bear?"

"Ah. Ah. Ah. I don't think so. I've never been a real bear. I don't have any claws. They wouldn't like me very much."

"I like you!" said Niall.

Susannah scowled and kicked the grass. It was true: real bears would probably not be kind to a transformed teddy bear.

"I guess it wasn't a good idea," Danny said. "But there must be something we can do."

Niall said, "You can come live with me, Mug. I'll play with you."

"Niall, don't be silly." Susannah was angry. *She* had met Mug first. "Where would you keep him?"

"In the bathroom."

"Mother won't let you keep a bear in the bathroom, stupid!"

Anansi said something swift and soft. Susannah watched Niall. He was trying to climb on the bear's back. Murgatroyd was smiling. Briefly Susannah wondered if Mother would let them keep a bear in the bathroom.

No. Definitely not.

Danielle whispered, "It's too bad he can't come with us. He isn't having any fun here."

"Murgatroyd," Mother Bea said, "how would you like to be a toy bear?"

"What?" the bear said.

"You don't wish to be a real bear. Shall I turn you into a toy again? If you say yes, I will send you into the far world with the children."

"Yeah!" Niall pummeled the bear's soft side. "Come be my toy."

"Hey," Susannah said.

"What is it?" asked Danielle.

Susannah looked at the ground. "It isn't fair."

"What's not fair?"

Susannah stuck her hands into her pockets. It was silly to feel bad because Niall had made friends with Murgatroyd. What would she do with a teddy bear? She was too old to play with toys. "Nothing. Never mind."

"Susannah," said the spider, "you need not be angry with Niall. You too are taking something out of Storyland."

"What?"

"You are wearing it."

Susannah touched her shirt. "It's just an old shirt," she muttered.

The spider sounded amused. "Nothing in Storyland is just an anything. Though your shirt is from your world, it was dipped in Mother Bea's cauldron. It carries a bit of magic with it."

"You mean it will be magic when I get home?"

"My lucky stone too?" said Danielle.

"I have said it," answered the spider enigmatically. Susannah frowned. Did that mean yes or no?

Niall was looking at her the way he looked at Mother when he really wanted something. Susannah beckoned to him. Docilely he slid from Murgatroyd's back and came to her.

"Niall," she said, "if Mug comes with us, will you promise always to be kind to him and to love him, cross your heart and hope to die?"

Niall crossed his heart. "I promise," he said. "Can I have him?"

"If he wants to come." She looked at Murgatroyd. The bear was wearing its most mournful expression. "Murgatroyd, would you like to come to our world and be a toy bear again?"

The bear rocked back and forth. Its brow furrowed. It bit its paws. It was thinking.

"Yes."

"Good," said Mother Bea. She twiddled her fingers in the air, and said something in magic. For a moment nothing happened. Then—Susannah gasped—Murgatroyd began to dwindle. He grew smaller and smaller.

Then there was only a small brown bear sitting stiffly in the

115

grass. Niall darted forward and picked it up. "Hello, Mug," he said, cradling the bear in his arms.

"Children, it's time for you to leave," said Mother Bea. "Hold hands." Susannah clasped Niall's right hand with her left. Danny reached for her right hand. "Now, walk toward the tree."

They walked. Mr. D. marched in front of them. The tree grew larger and larger. Beyond it the rising sun blazed into their eyes.

They stepped into the shadow of the tree.

"Good-bye!" Sarah called.

"Good-bye!" yelled Francis. "Sweet dreaming!"

"Good-bye," Susannah and Danny called together. Tree and grass and shadow and sun whirled around them. Susannah tightened her grip on Niall's hand. Her feet left the ground. She, Danny, Niall and the cat were flying—or were they falling—through a brilliant blue light. Susannah's stomach bounced. I *won't* be sick, she thought; people are never sick in stories, never!

The brightness turned black. Niall yelled. Susannah tried to call to him, to reassure him, but the air rushing past them blew her words away. She drew a deep breath and hollered.

"Hold on!"

Jeanne Gomoll

Chapter Eleven

They landed in the park.
Lying on her back, Susannah breathed deeply and waited for the
world to stop spinning. Fog—not enchanted mist, but moist, tangy
San Francisco fog—drifted over trees and benches and made halos
around the street lights. She turned her head. Niall lay with his

head resting on his arms, a brown teddy bear tucked to his chest. He snored. She turned the other way. Danielle was sitting cross-legged on the grass.

The girls gazed at each other. "Well, we're home," Danielle said. She began to pick grass stems from her hair and clothing. "Ugh, I'm wet."

"Me too," said Susannah. She heard a familar sound. She sat up. "Listen!" The red and yellow streetcar slid from the mouth of the tunnel and slithered down the street beside the park. Susannah grinned with relief. The streetcar looked and sounded the same as always. The park was the same; so was the street, and the silent, vigilant houses. She had been afraid that while they were absent from it their world had changed, the way Francis's world had changed.

But it had not.

"Merow." Mr. D stood just out of reach. His tail waved gently. His eyes were huge.

"Hello, cat." Susannah said. Stretching her arms to the sky, she yawned. Her eyes felt scratchy. The cat stared at her. Leaning forward, she stared at him. I guess he thinks it's time we were in bed.

Suddenly she wanted nothing more than the warmth of her own bed and well-known smells and shadows of her room.

She bent over Niall. "Niall," she whispered, "wake up." She had to say it several times before he opened his eyes. He blinked, staring at her and at the dark, empty park with bewilderment.

"Susannah? I want to go home."

"We're going home," Susannah said. "We're almost there. We're in the park. Stand up, Niall. You have to walk."

Naill stood. He cradled the brown bear in his arms. Susannah put a hand on the back of his pajama top. It was soaked. A breeze blew. He shivered. "I'm cold," he said.

"I know."

"I'm cold too, Niall," Danny said. She stood. Susannah looked for the moon but it had fallen behind the hills.

"You think anyone will be looking for us?" Danny sounded nervous.

"No." Susannah tried to sound more certain than she was. "They don't, in stories."

They crossed the streetcar tracks. Most of the houses on Allan Street were dark. One or two had lights gleaming behind their window shades, as if, Susannah thought, the houses had known that someone was going to be out late that night.

Maybe the houses had known.

"You know," Danny said, "we can't ever tell anyone about this. They'd think we were sick."

Susannah nodded. "Bizarro."

"We should do that thing that people do in stories when they promise not to tell stuff."

"They swear an oath."

"Yeah. Can we do it?"

"I think so." It was true; they should do something.

"How do we do it?"

"Hold hands," Susannah said. Danny gripped her fingers. "Say after me: I promise not to tell anyone about my adventure in Storyland."

Danielle repeated it. Niall, yawning, staggered against Susannah's leg. His eyes were shut.

She put a hand out to steady him. "Hey. Don't fall."

He grunted. "I think he's asleep," Danny said. She shivered.

"You better go." Susannah squinted at the dark windows of Danielle's house. "How will you get into your house?"

"Climb," said Danny. She grinned. Her teeth and eyes glittered. "I left the back door open. I'll climb the fence and go up the back stairs." She opened her arms wide. They hugged. Danny patted Niall lightly on the head. "Good night, Niall," she said. "See you tomorrow."

"I think it is tomorrow," Susannah said. She watched Danny cross the street cattycorner and lope to her house. Danielle halted to wave. Then, silent and fluid as a shadow, she went up and over the fence.

"Merow!" said Mr. D impatiently. He lashed his tail.

"Okay, okay, we're coming." Susannah followed the cat along the sidewalk. No one seemed awake on Allan Street. They reached the house. Susannah dragged the half asleep Niall up the steps. She tried to steer him around the creaky places. Mr. D waited on the top step. His fur was fluffed.

Susannah reached for the doorknob.

It was hard to turn.

She pushed. The door opened. Mr. D scooted inside. Susannah guided Niall in. The hall was wonderfully warm, and it smelled of the spaghetti Mother had made for dinner. They slipped by the big bedroom. Susannah's heart pounded.

Niall fell into bed. It's easy for him, Susannah thought, he's already wearing pajamas. She tugged at her tennis shoes and socks. It was really a hassle to take off all her clothes. But she made herself undress and put her clothes away. The sheets were cool. She wriggled into them, wriggling her toes to find the end of the bed. She felt a thump.

"Hello, Mr. D."

The big cat circled and folded himself against her feet.

"It was a neat Adventure, wasn't it?"

Purr.

"I bet cats have adventures all the time."

Purr.

"I want to remember it. I remember the broken dolls—and the magician in the tree—and the Lady—and Francis. I wonder what will happen to Francis—" She rubbed her tired eyes. Patterns whirled behind her eyelids. They reminded her of the jewels in the painted tunnel.

* * *

It was morning.

"Where is everybody?" The voice was her father's. He was yelling from the kitchen. Susannah opened her eyes. Ugh. They felt as if she had rubbed sand into them. The sun blazed in through the eastern window, spreading light like butter on the yellow walls. Susannah sniffed. Yum. She smelled eggs, bacon, and onions.

Niall was still asleep. Susannah propped herself on one elbow and stared at him, frowning. She had dreamed a complicated dream. He had been in it. So had Danielle.

Footsteps pounded in the hall. The bedroom door opened; her father came in. His hair stood up on his head in curls. It did that especially in the morning. "Hey," he said, leaning over her, "what's with you kids this morning?"

Susannah yawned. "I'm sleepy," she said with dignity.

"I'll say you are." He was a brown man: his skin was brown from the sun, his hair was brown, his eyes were brown. "You plan to spend the rest of the day in bed? Better not. I'll eat all the onions. No onions for Suzy, no onions for Niall." Singing, he left the room. He even had a brown voice. Susannah stretched her legs, trying to find the warm hollow that Mr. D sometimes left behind him. There it was. She let her toes bask in it for a moment.

It had been, she thought, a wonderful dream. The details had faded, but she remembered a bright full moon and a cave with icicles hanging from the ceiling. She wondered if she could make a picture of it. Her stomach fizzed, telling her that *it* was hungry even if she wasn't. Slowly she got out of bed and dressed. She had to fish under the bed for her tennis shoes. They were wet, which was odd, and they were covered with grass stems, which was really odd because she had not gone to the park the day before—had she?

Daddy was singing in the kitchen: a real song, not a made-up song. Susannah tied her shoelaces. Niall was out of it: his eyes were shut, and his arms were wrapped protectively around his teddy bear. Susannah frowned. Since when did Niall have a teddy bear? But there it was. It had black button eyes and its name was

Mug, short for Murgatroyd. Hunching her shoulders, she stared at it.

"Susannah," her father yelled, "I *will* eat the onions if you don't get up!"

"I'm up!" Rising, she went to the bathroom to wash her face and hands and comb her hair.

There were eggs and toast and butter and milk on the table in the kitchen. Mother was pouring coffee. She was wearing one of her dresses that was all one color. Daddy called them her tents. This one was blue.

"Good morning, Susie-pooh," she said. Her hair was undone; it fell around her face like a yellow curtain. "Did you sleep well?"

"Okay." Susannah went to kiss her. The mound of her belly poked out of the tent. Susannah touched it. Yesterday the baby had kicked. Was it—David or Corinna—impatient to come out? Maybe it was.

She patted the baby under the mound. Then she slid into her chair. Her father grinned at her. "You're a little somnambulist this morning," he said. It was a game he played with her, to use a word she didn't know and let her try to figure out what it meant. But this morning she didn't feel like playing. She drank her milk, very slowly; then she ate her bacon and eggs. She picked the onions out and pushed them to the side of the plate. They were her favorite bits, so she liked to eat them last.

Daddy told a story about someone on the bus last night. Usually Susannah listened to her father's stories. Today she could not seem to pay attention. Suddenly he tapped the table in front of her. "Susannah, you sick or something?"

"No," Susannah said, swallowing a mouthful of onions. "I was thinking about a dream."

Mother said, "What kind of dream?"

Susannah shrugged. "Just a dream."

"It must have been more than just a dream," Mother said. "Was it a pleasant dream?"

Daddy put his fork down hard on his plate, *bang*. "Bonnie, let the kid keep her dreams to herself."

"I thought she might want to talk about it," Mother said calmly. "She could learn to direct her dreams."

"So she could do what with them?" Daddy said. He was getting that special look on his face. Mother called it "argument mode." Mother was looking stubborn. Susannah took her plate and glass to the sink and ran water over them.

"Susannah, you didn't eat your toast."

"I don't want it," Susannah said. Her stomach had stopped fizzing. "Niall can have it."

"I bet Rembrandt ate all his toast when he was a little boy," Daddy said. Rembrandt, Susannah knew, was a painter.

"And I bet Van Gogh didn't," Mother answered.

A door banged down the hall. Susannah leaned on the refrigerator. Niall shuffled into the kitchen. He was carrying the teddy bear under one arm. He climbed into his chair. Mother put eggs on his plate.

"Good morning," Daddy said.

Niall squinted and mumbled.

"Did you have good dreams last night, Niall?" Mother asked.

Niall nodded. "Went to Storyland," he said.

"That's nice," said Mother. "Did you decide what to name your birthday bear?"

Susannah scowled. You have to name your toys, Mother had said, or else they run away to the Land of Runaway Toys. Yes.

Then why did that question seem so wrong to her?

Mother had been talking about the toy Celie had given Niall for his birthday. But Celie had gotten Niall a horse—a silver horse—*the* Silver Horse—for his birthday. Not a bear!

Susannah's heart was pounding so hard that she almost missed Niall's answer.

"His name is Murgatroyd."

Daddy chuckled. "That's a jawbreaker. Where'd you get that name?"

"In Storyland," Niall said. He sucked his teeth and held out his plate to Mother. "More eggs."

"Niall, don't make that noise with your teeth," Mother said, "it's disgusting." She put more eggs on his plate. "Eat your toast."

"Okay."

"When you want something, say please."

Susannah put her palm against the smooth cool surface of the refrigerator. Had everyone forgotten the Silver Horse but her? Was she crazy? Sicko? She closed her eyes. She could see it clearly, standing on the purple toy chest in the moonlight, glittering. . . .

Wham. Wham! Someone knocked on the front door.

"I wonder who that is," Mother said. "Susannah, would you see?"

Susannah went to the front door. She was too short to use the peephole, so she had to yell through the door. "Who is it?"

"It's me. Danny."

Susannah opened the door. Danny stood in the doorway. "Susannah, who is it?" Mother called.

"It's Danielle!"

"Well, don't stand in the doorway. Close the door."

Susannah closed the door. Danielle's hair was wild. "I need to talk to you," she said. Her voice was tight, as if her throat were sore, or as if she were angry.

"Okay." They walked to Susannah's room. Danielle sat on the bed. Niall's blue pajamas lay in a crumpled heap on his bed. Susannah picked them up to move them so that she could sit there.

They were damp.

Slowly Susannah sat. Danny said, "I had this dream last night. You were in it."

"I had a dream last night," Susannah said. "You were in it."

"I dreamed about a Silver Horse."

"And a witch in a wood."

124

"And broken dolls—and a Hill of Dreams—" Their words tumbled over each other.

"And a magician in a tree—"

"Yeah," Danielle said. "Niall was in it too. And the cat."

Susannah nodded. "Remember Francis?" she whispered. "And the harpies?"

"When I woke up this morning—" Danielle pulled her lucky stone over her head and held it on one palm—"I found *this*."

"Oh, wow," Susannah said.

Danielle's lucky stone had changed. It had been a solid gray. Now it was white, shot through with streaks of glitter.

"It's different," Danny said. "It wasn't like that before."

Susannah touched the stone with a finger. Suddenly she knew. It hadn't been a dream. It had happened. The Silver Horse was gone, and in its place was Murgatroyd. No one remembered the horse except her and Danny and maybe Niall. . . .

Niall walked in. The bear was under his arm. He looked at Danny and Susannah and at the white, sparkling stone between them, and grinned.

Susannah took a deep breath. "Niall—do you remember the Silver Horse?"

Niall looked at her as if she were crazy. "Uh huh."

"Where is it?"

"In Storyland."

He did remember! "Niall," Danny said, "you know that's a secret, don't you?"

"Uh huh," he said. Yawning, he put the bear on his right shoulder. "We're going to watch cartoons." He went out.

Down the hall the telephone rang.

Mother answered it. "Celie," she said, "hello!" Danny sat up straight, grimacing. "You know that your daughter is—what?" There was an ominous pause. Her voice lifted. "Danielle!"

"Uh oh," Danny said. "Yes'm!"

Mother came to the doorway. "That was your mother," she said to

Danny. "She says your room is the nastiest thing she's seen in months, and you better get right home and clean it up before you do anything else."

"Okay," Danny said. She rose. "Are you going to paint today?" she said to Susannah. "Can I watch?"

"No painting until the dishes get done!"

"Yes," Susannah said to them both. She didn't mind. The pictures were in her head, and they would stay there until she needed them. The Silver Horse jumped in the moonlight. The trees in the forest made black streaks against the light. A bare, brown hill floated like an island in fog.

She walked Danny to the door. "Come over later."

"I will." Danny hurtled down the steps. She paused at the bottom to wave.

Susannah waved back. I won't forget, she thought. Niall has a bear. I have a magic shirt. A talking door winked at me. She giggled, remembering Mother Bea's magic dishwasher pot. I wonder, she thought, if people ever get to go back to Storyland.

Then she walked into the kitchen, where the dishes waited to be washed.